THE IMMACULATE DECEPTION

IAIN PEARS

SCRIBNER

New York   London   Toronto   Sydney

SCRIBNER
1230 Avenue of the Americas
New York, NY 10020

Originally published simultaneously in the U.S. by Scribner and the UK by HarperCollins

First Scribner trade paperback edition 2005

SCRIBNER and design are trademarks of Macmillan Library Reference USA, Inc.,
used license by Simon & Schuster, the publisher of this work.

For information about special discounts for bulk purchases,
please contact Simon & Schuster Special Sales:
1-800-456-6798 or business@simonandschuster.com.

DESIGNED BY ERICH HOBBING

Set in Garamond No. 3

Manufactured in the United States of America

1   3   5   7   9   10   8   6   4   2

Library of Congress Control Number: 2001267391

ISBN 0-7432-1257-6
0-7432-7241-2 (Pbk)

To Michael and Alexander

THE
IMMACULATE
DECEPTION

I

One morning, a fine May morning in Rome, when the sun was beaming through the clouds of carbon monoxide and dust and giving a soft, fresh feel to the day, Flavia di Stefano sat immobile in a vast traffic jam that began in the Piazza del Popolo and ended somewhere near the Piazza Venezia. Many people, at least those with a different personality from her own, would have been unperturbed by this common occurrence, and would instead have contemplated their surroundings with something approaching patient smugness. Not many, after all, can call on a Mercedes, complete with chauffeur and obligatory tinted windows, to ferry them around town at the taxpayers' expense. Fewer still at such a young age are the head (if only the *acting* head) of one of the more reputable departments in the Italian police force, complete with its own budget, personnel, and expense accounts.

And virtually none of the small number of departmental potentates use their splendid forms of transport to go to unspecified meetings, called late the previous evening, at the Palazzo Chigi, the official residence of the Italian prime minister.

That, of course, was the problem, and the reason behind Flavia's insensitivity to the early morning sunshine, and her disdain for all living things. For a start, her collar itched monstrously, and was a permanent, nagging reminder of her own inexperience and desire to

1

create the right impression. Instead of sitting quietly that morning eating toast and drinking coffee, she had run around showering, choosing clothes, and worst of all, applying copious amounts of makeup. Then having a fit of defiance and taking it all off again, then weakening with nerves and putting it all back on. Worse still, she stood peering out of the window into the little piazza below, anxiously waiting for the car to arrive, checking and rechecking the contents of her handbag. She had nightmare visions of grabbing her coat and running through the streets of Rome to get there. Breaking a heel on a cobblestone. Arriving out of breath, her hair in a mess. Creating entirely the wrong impression. Career destroyed, over in a moment, just because some damn fool driver didn't turn up. And what was more, she felt ill; stomach in a turmoil, the rest of her queasy. Bug. Flu, probably. Nervousness. Something like that. It was going to be one of those days. She knew it.

"Flavia. Do stop jiggling about like that. You're making me nervous." Jonathan Argyll, her husband of four weeks' standing, and boyfriend-cum-flatmate of near ten years, sat at the kitchen table trying to read the newspaper. "It's only the prime minister, you know."

Flavia turned around to scowl at him.

"I'm not being facetious," he went on calmly as he reached for the marmalade before she could tell him what she thought of his sense of whimsy. "You know as well as I do that bad news is always handed out by underlings. Besides, you haven't done anything wrong recently, have you? Not misplaced a Raphael, dropped a Michelangelo, shot a senator, or anything?"

Another scowl.

"There you are, then. Nothing to worry about," he continued, getting up to give her a quick pat to indicate that he sympathized. "Even less now that your car has arrived."

He pointed downward, waved cheerfully at the driver, whom he vaguely recognized, and even more cheerfully at Flavia, as she rushed for her bag and coat.

"Calm. Remember?" he said as she opened the door.

"I remember."

Calm, she repeated to herself thirty minutes later as she looked at her watch one more time. Stuck in a traffic jam, half a mile to go, five minutes late. At least it cut the unaccustomed car sickness. Calm, she thought.

It was Bottando's fault, really, she reflected. Her erstwhile boss, now gone on to greater things, was one of those who liked formulating universal laws about life, which he delivered as aphorisms that came back to haunt you at inappropriate moments.

"Politicians," he said once over a glass of brandy following a long lunch. "Politicians can ruin your day. Ministers, on the other hand, can ruin your week."

"And prime ministers?" Flavia had asked.

"Prime ministers? Oh, they can ruin your life."

His little bon mot, for some reason, didn't seem quite so urbane at the moment. She considered leaning forward to see if the driver could go any faster, but abandoned the idea. Another one of Bottando's rules. Never let anyone see you are nervous—especially not drivers, who are notoriously the biggest gossips on the planet. So, like a condemned man who finally realizes his fate is inevitable, she gave a big sigh, leaned back, and gave up fretting. Immediately, the lights changed, the cars began moving, and the palazzo came into sight. She was waved through the vast wooden gates into the courtyard with virtually no delay, and within minutes was being ushered into an anteroom to an anteroom to the office where Antonio Sabauda, prime minister now for a whole nine months, held his audiences. Fourteen minutes late.

Her guardian angel was on duty, working hard on her behalf. Sabauda was later still, and over the next forty minutes she allowed herself to work up a fine head of steam about the lack of consideration shown by unpunctual people. In fact, by the time the door was finally opened and she was shown in, the nervousness was gone, the deference dissipated, the stomach quiescent, and her character quite restored to its normal state.

So she marched into the surprisingly dingy office thinking only how stupid she had been to put on quite so much lipstick and wishing she hadn't bothered, shook hands with the prime minister in a uninterested fashion, and sat down on a chair before she was asked. What did she care? She hadn't voted for him.

He scored early points by referring neither to her age, nor to the fact that she was a woman, and pushed his rating even higher by not indulging in any small talk. Then he spoiled it all by expressing surprise that Bottando himself had not come. Flavia reminded him that she, not General Bottando, was now running the art theft squad on a day-to-day basis.

"But he is still the head of it, is he not?"

"Nominally. But he takes no active role in our operations anymore. He is running this European venture, and that uses up all his time."

"And more of his patience," the prime minister added for her with a faint smile. "I see. And I am sure we are in safe hands with you, signora. I do hope so anyway. I'm afraid there is something of a crisis on hand. I would tell you about it myself, but I know few of the details. Dottore Macchioli knows those, and he has just arrived. This, I'm afraid, is why you have been kept waiting for so long."

Of course, Flavia thought. All is now clear. Alessandro Macchioli was one of those endearingly lovable characters who sows disaster everywhere he goes. Never on time for anything, however much he tried, always colliding with all manner of inanimate objects that leapt out at him as he passed, he was the very model of the unworldly scholar. And as a scholar he was very fine indeed, so Jonathan told her, as he knew more about this sort of thing than she did. But as the director of the National Museum, he was, in Bottando's opinion, one of the wonders of the world. His elevation had come on the rebound; his predecessor had been go-getting, dynamic, determined to drag the musty museum into modernity, and was shortly to be let out of jail. The embarrassment had been considerable, and Macchioli—who could not only resist temptation but probably wouldn't even notice he was being tempted—had seemed the obvious successor, in the circumstances. A safe pair of hands; back to the traditional values of connoisseurship, erudition, and old-time curating. A universally beloved figure, in fact, but quite incapable of defending his patch against the incursions of bureaucrats who wished to cut his funds, to ooze up to potential benefactors, or to manage his disorganized museum.

And deeply unhappy, Flavia judged from the nervous way he came in, thrusting his bicycle clips into the bulging pocket of his shabby suit. It was all most intriguing.

Macchioli sat down, fiddled with his hands, and looked uncomfortable as the introductions were made.

"Perhaps we might begin?" the prime minister prompted.

"Ah, yes," Macchioli said absently.

"You have a problem that you wish to tell the signora about?"

Persuading himself to divulge it was evidently a titanic struggle, almost as though he knew that, once he had spoken, all sorts of unpleasant consequences might begin to swirl around him. He rocked to and fro, hunched his shoulders, rubbed his nose, and then, in a sudden burst of decision, spoke: "I've lost a picture. The museum has. It was stolen."

Flavia was puzzled. She could see why he was upset. Awkward business, losing pictures. That was not the problem, however. They went missing all the time; so often, in fact, that the routine for what to do was well established. You phoned the police. They went around, did their stuff and then you forgot all about it, on the reasonable grounds that the picture was unlikely ever to be seen

5

again. All perfectly normal. It was hearing about it in the prime minister's office that was not entirely orthodox.

"I see," she said helpfully, but poor old Macchioli did not take it as a prompt to continue; instead he lapsed into another agonized silence.

"For the last five years, you see, we have been planning an exhibition." He restarted, evidently deciding that a sidelong approach might be best. "To celebrate Italy's presidency of the European Community, which begins in fifteen days' time. Drawing on all aspects of European art, but I am afraid that *some* people"—and here he gave a surreptitious glance in the direction of the desk at which the prime minister was sitting—"*some* people have sought to turn it into a nationalistic demonstration."

"Just a small reminder of our contribution in matters of culture," the prime minister purred.

"This has made borrowing the works a little more difficult than it might have been," Macchioli continued. "Not that it is relevant to the disaster that has befallen us . . ."

The prime minister, showing more patience than his reputation would have suggested possible, sighed in the background. It was enough to bring Macchioli's errant mind back to the immediate issue.

"We did, however, finally arrange to borrow nearly all the paintings we wanted. Most from Italian institutions, naturally, but a good proportion from foreign museums and owners. Many of the pictures have never been seen in this country before."

"But I know about all this," said Flavia with more impatience than the prime minister was showing. "We've been involved in the planning for years. Members of my department escorted the first few paintings from the airport to the museum last week."

"Yes. And a very fine job you did, too. No mistake about that. Very fine. Unfortunately . . ."

"The one you've had stolen. It was one of those?"

He nodded.

"When?"

"Yesterday. At lunchtime."

"Lunchtime? Then why are you only telling me about it now?"

"It was very awkward, you see. I wasn't at all sure what to do about it . . ."

"Perhaps I might fill the signora in?" The prime minister interrupted, glancing at his watch and realizing that, unless something was done soon, this meeting might last for the rest of the day and Macchioli still wouldn't have explained anything. "Please correct me if I get the details wrong. I understand the picture was stolen at around half past one yesterday. A hooded man reversed a truck into the storage area, held up the people working there, forced them to load the painting, complete with its frame, into the back of the truck, and drove off. Is that correct?"

Macchioli nodded.

Flavia, fidgeting around in her seat, opened her mouth to make the obvious protests about wasted time, trails going cold, and so on.

"Your department, signora, was not called because the thief left behind a message saying that the police should not be contacted."

"A ransom demand, is that it?"

A shrug. "Not exactly. Just that we'd be hearing more in due course. I suppose that means money."

"Maybe so. What, exactly, is the picture?"

"It's a Claude Lorrain. *Landscape with Cephalus and Procris,*" Macchioli said reluctantly.

Flavia paused. "Oh, not *that* one, surely? Not the one where the government intervened officially to guarantee it?"

He nodded. You could see why he was upset, she thought. Not that it was such a great picture, although she always found Claude quite toothsome. Not a Raphael, or anything like that. But it had such a dodgy past. Its reputation as one of the most stolen pictures in the world ensured it a status beyond its simple quality. Argyll, no doubt, would remember the details better than she could, but she could recall the highlights. Painted in the 1630s for an Italian cardinal. Pinched by the duke of Modena when he found it in a wagon after a battle. Pinched again by a French general a few years later. Looted and sold during the French Revolution, pinched again by Napoleon when he came across it in Holland. Stolen by thieves in the 1930s, by the Germans in the 1940s, and by two more thieves in the 1950s and 1960s. Whereupon the exasperated owner sold it to the Louvre, in the hope that they would manage to hang on to it. Which they had. Until, it seemed, it had arrived in Italy.

"Oh, dear," she said.

"You see our problem," the prime minister continued. "It is exceptionally unpleasant for me, as I gave a personal guarantee about its safety. Quite apart from that, this exhibition is to be one of the cultural high points of our presidency. It would be very bad indeed if it was wrecked, and it would be wrecked if this news gets out. It is quite possible that other lenders would pull out, and even if they didn't our reputation would be damaged badly. You can imagine what would be said. We would look quite ridiculous."

Flavia nodded. "So? When you get the ransom demand you pay up."

"The only problem is that it is illegal. If we arrest people for paying ransoms to rescue their wives and children, we can hardly pay up for a mere painting."

A silence fell on the room, and it seemed as though Flavia was expected to say something useful.

"You mean you want me to find the painting?"

"I would ordinarily be deeply grateful, but in this case, no. How many people would you use for such an inquiry?"

Flavia thought for a moment. "Everyone we had, if you wanted a quick result. Not that I can guarantee one."

"And could you at least guarantee to keep it out of the press?"

"For about six hours, yes."

"Precisely. Secrecy in this matter is absolutely vital. Even if you were successful and recovered the painting swiftly, the damage would still be done."

"In which case, I confess to being defeated. You won't pay a ransom and won't look for the painting. What, exactly, do you want done?"

"*We* cannot pay a ransom. The *government* cannot authorize such a thing. *Taxpayers'* money cannot be used. Nor can any government employee be involved in its payment. Do I make myself clear?"

He did. But Flavia had not spent years watching Bottando take avoiding action without learning a thing or two.

"I'm afraid I'm not with you at all. Sorry," she said blandly.

"You will use your best abilities to recover this painting without any publicity. But I must make it absolutely clear that I cannot and will not condone the payment of a ransom from *public* funds."

"Ah."

"Should these criminals be paid off independently from a private source, a man willing to break the law for what he considers erroneously the public good, then that, of course, I cannot prevent, much though I might regret it."

"I see."

"You will keep me informed every day about your investigation, and will receive instructions as you proceed. Might I also say that the need for secrecy is absolute."

"You are rather tying my hands here."

"I'm sure you will manage."

"And if I come across any other way of recovering this picture?"

"You will restrain yourself. I want no risk of all of this coming into the open." He stood up. "I think that is all for the time being. Let me know of your progress every day, if you please."

Two minutes later, both Flavia and Macchioli were in an anteroom once more, she a little perplexed about the whole business, the museum director seemingly lost in despondency.

"Right, then," she said after a while. "I think you need to tell me a little more about what on earth has been going on here."

"Hmm?"

"Robbery? Armed man? Remember?"

"Yes, yes. What do you want to know?"

"How about how to contact this person? If I am to hand over money to them in some way, I ought to know how to set about it."

Macchioli looked blank. "What do you mean, hand over money? I thought you had just been told that you were to do no such thing?"

She sighed. The trouble with Macchioli was that there was no disingenuousness about him at all. He really did think that they had just sat through a meeting and been given instructions that no money was to be paid. That, of course, might well turn into a major problem.

"Doesn't matter. Forget it," she said. "This message, it gave no means of contact?"

"No."

"Can I see it, please?"

"It's in my office."

It was like talking to a particularly stupid child. "Why don't we go to your office, then?"

"There," he said, forty minutes later, after a silent voyage through the streets of Rome. "It's not very informative."

Flavia took the piece of paper—no point in worrying about fingerprints or anything like that now—and looked. True enough. She could hardly fault the analysis. Six words only. She even admired the economy of expression.

She leaned back in her seat and thought. Did it tell her anything? "You'll be hearing from me." Done on a computer printer, but who didn't have access to one these days? The paper was standard-issue computer paper, of which there were several billion sheets consumed every day. No, it told her nothing; or, at least, nothing that the author didn't want her to know.

"The robbery itself," she said, turning her attention back to Macchioli.

He shook his head. "Very little to say you haven't already been told. A small truck; the sort that traders use to deliver fruit and vegetables. A man dressed up as Leonardo da Vinci . . ."

"What?" she asked incredulously. He had said it as though people dressed as Renaissance painters or baroque popes were to be seen pottering about the museum every day.

"One of those masks you buy in party shops. You know. And a sort of cape. And the gun, of course. Do you want to see that?"

She looked at him wearily. Mere expressions of incredulity seemed inadequate somehow. "The gun?"

"He dropped it when he drove off. Threw it, actually. At the men who helped him load the picture. This was after he handed out chocolates."

"Chocolates?" she said weakly.

"Little boxes of chocolates. Belgian ones, I believe. You know, the ones that you buy in specialty shops. With a ribbon on the top."

"Of course. Where are they?"

"What?"

"The chocolates."

"The guards ate them."

"I see. Blood sugar levels low because of the shock, no doubt. Apart from that, no violence of any sort?"

"No."

"I'd like to talk to these people in the storeroom."

"You'll have to."

"What do you mean?"

"Someone has to tell them to keep quiet about this."

"You haven't done that?"

"Of course. But nobody ever listens to me."

11

Flavia sighed. "Very well, then. Take me to them. Then you can show me the gun."

She decided on the brutal approach. Not simply because it was one of those days, and she wasn't feeling in the mood for subtleties, but because she knew that being young and a woman meant that it was sometimes difficult to persuade people—especially the sort of people who unload paintings—to take her seriously.

"Right," she said, when the two men had come in and sat down. "I will say this once and once only. I am the head of the art theft squad, investigating the theft of this picture. You two are prime suspects. Got that?"

They didn't answer but, judging by the way they turned a little pale, she assumed they had.

"I want it back fast, and more important people than myself want there to be no publicity. If there is any, if anyone hears about what has happened here, and I trace it back to you two, I will personally ensure (a) that you go to jail for aiding and abetting a crime, (b) that you stay in jail for conspiracy to pervert the course of justice, (c) I will have you fired from this job, and (d) I will ensure that neither of you ever gets a job again. Is that understood?"

More pallor.

"In order to avoid this regrettable fate, all you have to do is keep your mouths shut. There was no theft, you know of no theft, nothing untoward happened yesterday. You may find that difficult, but you will find the self-discipline rewarding. Do I make myself absolutely clear?"

She was rather proud of the speech, delivered with all the cold conviction of a true apparatchik, able to call on untold occult powers to visit terrible consequences on the innocent. Anyone would have seen it was all nonsense after a moment's thought, and that there was nothing she could do to them at all, but the two men seemed too dull to notice. She only hoped they were not so dull that they failed to grasp what she wanted of them.

That would become clear in the next few days; what was immediately apparent, alas, was that they were certainly too dim-witted to be much use as witnesses. Their description of the robbery was scarcely more detailed than the brief summary that Macchioli and Sabauda had already given her. The only facts they added was that the van was large enough to get a Claude in, was white, and wasn't a Fiat. The man involved was of average height and might (or might not) have had a Roman accent. She dismissed them after twenty minutes with another dire warning, then was taken to see the gun.

Macchioli was keeping it in his safe. In a plastic bag. He was inordinately proud of himself about the plastic bag.

"There," he said, putting it gingerly on his desk. "We were lucky it didn't go off when it hit the ground."

Flavia felt like weeping. Some days were just so abominable she didn't know how she stood it. She took out her handkerchief, picked up the gun, looked at it for a few moments, then pointed it at her head.

"Signora! Be careful!" shouted Macchioli in alarm.

She looked at him sadly, closed her eyes, and to the older man's horror, slowly pulled the trigger.

The sound of what was later identified by analysts—or rather by a secretary in payroll, who was an opera enthusiast—as a jaunty version of Verdi's "Teco io sto. Gran Dio!" from Act Two of *Un Ballo in Maschera*, rendered on a little widget buried deep inside the gun's handle, drifted slowly across the room.

Flavia opened her eyes, shrugged, and tossed the gun onto the desk.

"If we manage to find a shop that has recently sold a Leonardo da Vinci mask and a plastic singing gun to a man carrying chocolates, we might have a lead," she said, as she put the gun back into the bag. "I'll let you know."

Five minutes later she was slumped in the back of the car, muttering darkly to herself. Then she reached a decision. Whatever injunctions other people needed to obey on keeping their mouths shut, she needed to ventilate. She gave her driver directions to head for the EUR.

2

Despite the morning, Flavia thought little on the journey or, at least, thought little about Claude and its inconvenient disappearance. Rather, she thought about her old boss, General Taddeo Bottando, poor soul, consigned to opulent exile in this grim suburb, surrounded by office blocks and 1930s architecture and wastelands where nothing much seemed to happen. He had been stuck out here for a year now, heading some grandiosely named European directive, as cut off from the mainstream of policing as his location suggested. Only bankers should have to work in this awful place; scarcely even a decent restaurant to go to at lunchtime, and Bottando was a man who liked his lunch.

Whereas the art squad building was run down but beautiful, underfunded but buzzing with activity, Bottando's new suburban empire was grand, dripping in cash but ugly and deathly quiet. Merely getting into the building required going through the sort of security procedures that usually defend classified government installations. Everybody was terribly well-dressed, the carpets were thick, the doors swished to and fro electrically, the computers hummed. A policeman's paradise, enough resources to tackle the world. Poor, poor man, she thought.

But Bottando put a brave face on it, and Flavia smiled encouragingly, both of them going through the ritual of pretending that all was well as they did on every occasion they met. He talked about the splendid things his new operation would shortly accomplish, she made joking remarks about European expense accounts. Neither ever referred to the fact that Bottando was showing his age just a bit more, that his conversation was just that touch duller, that his jokes and good humor were now ever so slightly forced.

Nor was his heart in it any longer; he was away more often than he was behind his desk, constantly, it seemed, taking holidays. Winding down. Preparing his exit. It was only a matter of time before the holiday became permanent. A couple of years and he would have to retire anyway, although while in his old post at the art theft squad he had fended off even the thought; there was nothing to retire to. He was one of those people whose very existence was inconceivable without his job and his position.

His promotion had lost him both, and maybe that was the intention. To ease him out by easing him up, and perhaps Bottando was ready to go; he would have fought the move more had he not been halfway there already. He had won bigger battles against greater odds in the past. Maybe he'd had enough.

Fairly often now, Flavia came to see him not because she wanted his advice but because she wanted him to give it. She had been running the art theft squad for a year and had settled in. Better still, she found she was good at it and no longer needed to be anybody's protégée. She had leaned on Bottando heavily in the earlier days, but needed to do so no longer. He had, she was sure, noticed this and was pleased for her. The last time he came to the department, a few months back to check some old files and gather some materials, she knew he was just checking to make sure all was well. She was also sure that the visit was for no real reason, and that he stayed most of the afternoon—wandering about, reading this and that, chatting to people in corridors, going out for a drink afterward—largely because he had so little of substance to do in his own offices. She only hoped that he didn't suspect that sometimes—just sometimes—she felt a little sorry for him.

This time, however, there was no artifice in her visit. She was entering dark and stormy waters, and needed a bit of navigational guidance. She half-knew already what the advice would be; she nonetheless still needed to hear it.

Bottando came out of his office to greet her, gave her an affectionate kiss, and fussed about making her comfortable.

"My dear Flavia, how pleasant to see you. Not often we have you out in the provinces like this. What can I do for you? I assume, that is, that you haven't come just to feast your eyes on a properly funded department?"

She smiled. "I always like to see how things should be done, of course. But, in fact, I am here for some more of your best vintage advice. *Premier cru,* if you please."

"Always willing to put age at the service of enthusiasm," he replied. "As you know. I hope it is a real problem this time, not just something constructed to make me feel less obsolete."

He had noticed. Damn. Flavia felt genuinely, truly remorseful.

"You once told me prime ministers can ruin your life," she said.

"So they can. Especially if you get in their way. What have you got to do with prime ministers?"

With a brief preface about injunctions placed on her for silence, she told him.

Bottando listened intently, scratched his chin, stared at the ceiling, and grunted as the tale progressed, just as he always had when they had talked over a problem in the old days. And as the story continued, Flavia saw the slightest gleam come into his eyes, like an old and battered flashlight given a new battery.

"Aaah," he said with satisfaction as she finished, leaning back in his chair and gorged on the tale. "I can quite see why you want a second opinion. Most interesting."

"Exactly. The first question that strikes me, of course, is why such interest from on high? I mean, urgent meetings with the prime minister because of a picture?"

"I suppose you have to take the explanation about the government's sensitivity toward the European presidency at face value," Bottando said thoughtfully. "If I remember, the prime minister wants to make law and order his top priority. Antonio Sabauda will have a hard time pontificating about security if everybody is sniggering at him behind their memoranda all the while. No politician likes to look silly. They're very touchy on the subject; that's why they confuse their egos with the national interest so often."

"Maybe. Nevertheless, it strikes me that should anything go wrong, and there is a good chance that it will, then I am in a somewhat exposed position."

"Nothing on paper, I take it?"

Flavia shook her head. Bottando nodded appreciatively.

"I thought not. And the only other person to hear what was said was old Macchioli. Who is as malleable as a piece of lead sheeting." More thought. "Let's say it goes wrong. Everything appears in the newspaper, big scandal. Indignant prime minister says that he gave you instructions personally to drop everything and recover the painting, yet you did nothing about it. Hmm?"

Flavia nodded.

"Even worse, news takes some time to get out. Same indignant prime minister expressing shock that a policewoman should go around raising cash from unnamed sources to pay a ransom."

Another nod. "I could go to prison for that."

"So you could, my dear. Two years, not counting anything that might be tagged on for corruption and conspiracy."

"And if everything goes well . . ."

"If everything goes well, and you get the picture back, you will have performed a sterling service, which no one will know about. But you will know that the prime minister—a man who has many enemies and who has been in political life so long his skills as a survivor should never be underestimated—connived to get around the law so he could look good strutting the international stage. Knowledge, sometimes, can be a dangerous thing. Were you more ruthless, you could perhaps apply a little pressure on him, but he is more likely to see you as an ever-present threat and take the appropriate action. Something subtle, so that if you ever said anything, the response could be along the lines of 'poor embittered woman, trying to create a fuss because she was dismissed for incompetence.' Or corruption, or gross indecency, or something like that. Enough to make sure no one took you seriously. As I say, prime ministers can ruin your life."

Flavia felt her heart sinking as he spoke. Everything he said she had known, of course; having it spelled out in quite such a bald fashion did not raise her morale.

"Recommendations?"

Bottando grunted. "More difficult. What are your options, now? A strategic but untraceable leak to the press, followed by a public promise on your part to leave no stone unturned, etcetera? It would eliminate the prospect of going to jail at some future date, but pretty much ensure that prime ministerial wrath would descend on you with full force. End of a promising career. Do as you are told? Bad idea, for obvious reasons, especially as Macchioli would say on oath that you had been specifically instructed not to pay a penny."

"Doesn't leave much, does it?"

"Not at the moment, no. Tell me, this ransom money, where is it to come from?"

"I have no idea. Maybe an extremely wealthy patriot will suddenly wander through the door with a checkbook."

"Stranger things have happened. Let us assume that the money turns up. What then?"

"Get the picture back. Then go after whoever was responsible. They might do it again, after all."

Bottando shook his head. "Bad idea. What you must do is keep your head down. Do as you are told, and nothing else."

"But I'm not sure what I have been told to do. That's the trouble."

"I am merely trying to indicate that, when faced with deviousness, you must be devious yourself. You might also consider the wisdom of putting everything down on paper in front of a lawyer, so that, if necessary, your understanding of the meeting is clear."

Flavia sniffed, in exactly the same manner as Bottando used to do himself when she had proposed a distasteful idea and he had acted the part of cautious superior. The general noticed the sound, and all it implied, and smiled gently. For he also, in his way, felt slightly sorry for Flavia. Position and authority were not without their disadvantages, and having to be careful and responsible were among the biggest.

"I don't suppose you would like to help . . ."

"Me?" Bottando chuckled. "Dear me no. I most certainly would not. I am too old, my dear, to be running around with suitcases full of money under my arm. Besides, I must plead self-interest."

"What do you mean?"

"I am bored, Flavia," he said mournfully. "Bored out of my head. I have been sitting here pushing little bits of paper around for a year. I give orders to people who give orders to people who do some policing occasionally but spend most of their time constructing international directives. So I have decided that enough is enough. I am going to retire. My pension will be very much less than I had anticipated but quite sufficient. And I do not want to risk it at the moment. I will willingly give you any advice you want. And when I am finally retired any assistance you want as well. But at the moment, I must keep my head down as much as you."

"I'm really sorry you're going," she said, suddenly afflicted by an enormous sense of panic and loss.

"You'll survive without me, I dare say. And my mind is quite made up. Even the most fascinating job palls after a while, and as you may have noticed, what I'm doing at the moment is not especially fascinating. By the way, those chocolates. Did you say Belgian?"

"Yes."

"Ah."

"Why?"

"No reason. Merely a detail. Always thought them overrated, myself."

She stood up, looking at her watch. Late, late, late. Was it always to be like this now? Constant meetings, constant rush? Never time to sit and talk anymore? After several decades of it, she'd be ready to give it all up as well. She gave Bottando a brief embrace, told him to keep himself ready to give more advice, and headed back to her car. The driver was sound asleep on the backseat, waiting for her. Lucky man, she thought as she prodded him awake.

3

She was home early, even before Jonathan, and drank a glass of wine on the terrace—her promotion, their marriage, and the fact that even Jonathan now had a regular salary of a sort meant that, finally, they could afford an apartment they were happy to be in. Still in Rome's Trastevere section, but four whole rooms now, high ceilings, and a terrace overlooking a quiet square. If you stretched you could just see a bit of Santa Maria. Flavia was too short, but Jonathan could see it, and it gave him a twinge of pleasure just to know it was there. Although the least house-proud of people, even she made something of an effort to keep the apartment neat and tidy. A sign of age, perhaps.

She had left early because she wanted some time to think, and there were always too many distractions in her office. Phones, secretaries, people popping in and out to ask her opinion, or to get her to sign something. She loved it all, most of the time, but it made it difficult to reflect and consider. That was best done looking out at the ocher-colored buildings opposite, watching people doing their shopping, listening to the quiet murmur of a city going about its business.

Bottando's lack of practical advice had given her more than a little to think about. She had gone through Bottando's response, backward and forward, considering every option and possibility in a methodical way, and come up with nothing better. However, the essence of it—keep your head down, do nothing but avoid any involvement—appalled her. And struck her as almost as dangerous as doing something. Her head was on the block, come what may. If something, anything, went wrong, she would be the one to take the blame. Acting head of the department. Never yet confirmed in her post, even after a year. A matter of a moment to get rid of her; no noise, no fuss. Simply an announcement that a new and permanent chief, more experienced and fitted for the job, was being drafted in over her.

But what could she do? It was certainly the case that she couldn't do anything practical without somebody finding out quickly. Nor could she go trotting around the wealthy of Italy asking if they had a spare suitcase full of unwanted dollars. Fund-raising was hardly her job. If anyone could do it, it should have been Macchioli's task. That's what museum directors did these days. Or were supposed to. Alas, his talents notoriously did not lie in this direction at all. Still, it might be worthwhile having a serious talk with him, just in case a ransom note arrived.

Argyll came home an hour later, in a relatively good mood considering he'd spent the day trying to din the rudiments of art history into his students, and plunked himself down beside her to admire the view. Once it had been as admired as was possible, he'd asked about the meeting with the prime minister. She didn't want to talk about it yet, so she fended him off.

"How's the paper?" she asked mischievously to take her mind off things. This was a sore point with Argyll. He had been taken on in his current job to teach baroque art to foreign students passing a year in Rome, a task he was eminently fitted to do. Then the adminstration—a baroque organization itself—had decided, for reasons that no one really understood, that salary levels would be partly determined by academic production as well as hours put in at the coal face. Raise the reputation of the institution. Must be taken seriously as a university, not dismissed as a finishing school for rich kids. Which, of course, it was. The essence of the edict, however, was that if you wanted more money, you had to produce articles. Papers. Better still, a book or two.

Not really that easy, and Argyll was of a stubborn disposition. The idea of being forced into writing academic works annoyed him. However, a bit more money would be agreeable. He was nearly there; he had ruthlessly exploited his old footnotes and conjured up two articles of extraordinary banality for minor journals, and had also been invited to give a paper at a conference in Ferrara in a few weeks' time, and that would put him over the threshold.

Except that he didn't have a paper to deliver and, while he did not hesitate to produce grandiose trivia in the comforting anonymity of a journal no one read, he hesitated to stand up in front of a live audience and parrot obvious nonsense. So no paper; not even the glimmer of one. He was beginning to get worried. Flavia did her best to sympathize when he told her, again, that he still couldn't think of anything, and eventually Argyll shifted to another topic, lest dwelling on the matter ruin an otherwise pleasant evening.

"I had a phone call today."

"Oh?"

"From Mary Verney."

She put down her drink and looked at him. Not today, she thought. It's been bad enough already without Mary Verney. She was retired, Flavia knew; she had said so the last time they almost arrested her for art theft on a grand scale. But she'd said that the time before last as well.

"She asked me to ask you if you'd mind if she came back to Italy."

"What?"

Argyll said it again. "She has a house somewhere in Tuscany, it seems. She hasn't felt comfortable going there for the last few years, what with you so keen to lock her up. So she simply wanted to know whether you had any outstanding business with her. If you do, she'll stay in England and sell the house, but if you don't she wouldn't mind coming and seeing if it still has a roof. I said I'd ask. Don't look at me like that," he concluded mildly. "I'm the messenger. You know, the one you don't shoot."

Flavia huffed. "I really do have better things to do, you know, than reassuring aging thieves."

"So it seems."

"What does that mean?" she snapped.

"You weren't really listening to my fascinating anecdote about the coffee machine in the staff room. My little joke about the tourist being taken to hospital when a piece of the Pantheon fell on his head didn't make you smile at all, even though it was quite a clever play on words and would normally have produced at least a flicker of amusement. And you have twice dipped your olive into the sugar bowl and eaten it without even noticing."

So she had. Now she thought about it, the olive had tasted odd. So she heaved a sigh and told him about more serious matters. By the time she finished, Argyll was dipping his olives in the sugar bowl as well. He, in contrast, found them quite tasty. He could see that Flavia's situation did really put the antics of the departmental percolator in the shade.

Oddly, the more important matter was swiftly dealt with. Flavia didn't want Argyll's advice on this one, but she got it anyway. It just wasn't very good. "Your stomach," he said. "It's been playing you up for days now. How about if we got Giulio downstairs to have you admitted to hospital for a week? Urgent tests? Suspected ulcer? Gastroenteritis? You could blame my cooking. He'd be happy to oblige. Then you could sit out the case of the stolen Claude in peace and security."

Giulio was the doctor who lived on the grander first floor of their apartment block. And Flavia was sure he would oblige. He was an obliging fellow. And her stomach—in fact, her entire internal system was misbehaving shockingly, although it was better now, probably thanks to the wine. But this was one case she could not duck out of, and Argyll knew it as well as she did.

"Don't be silly," she said. "If you want to be useful, you can tell me about this Claude picture."

"What's to tell? It's a landscape. Not one of his huge ones, which is no doubt why it's so popular with the thieves."

"What about the subject, though? Cephalus and Procris."

Argyll waved his hand dismissively. "Wouldn't worry about that. They're just mythological figures wandering around the canvas who were put in to give it respectability. Claude couldn't do people for toffee. Arms and legs too long. Bums in the wrong place. But he had to do them to be taken seriously."

"Still. What's the story?"

"No idea."

And Flavia clearly wanted to say no more, so he switched the topic. "Tell me about Bottando. You'll miss him, won't you?"

"Terribly. Father figure, you know. It gives you a shock when permanent fixtures are suddenly not so permanent. Also, he's not happy about retiring, either. It's not a good way to end his career after all this time."

"We should get him a present."

She nodded. "Can you think of anything?"

"No."

"Nor me."

They paused. "What shall I do about Mary Verney?" Argyll said.

She sighed. "Oh, I don't know. I suppose there are so many thieves in the country, one more won't make any difference. At least we can be certain she didn't steal the Claude."

4

Argyll was reluctant to criticize his dear wife, especially as she had been his wife for only a short time and it seemed premature to begin carping, but he found it hard to suppress a certain amount of irritation at the way she wouldn't listen to reason—his reason—about this Claude. It was not that he didn't see that it was her job to recover pictures, nor did he blame her for being worried. Normally it was her calm that amazed him. He knew well that he would have been quite incapable of doing what she did without being in a permanent state of panic. The omnipresent possibility of disaster that she seemed to live with was not the sort of thing that gave him pleasure; in his own line of work, now that being an art dealer was more of a hobby than an occupation, the worst that could happen was that he might lose his lecture notes. Selling his remaining stock of pictures and covering his expenses was more than enough stress to have in his life, in his opinion.

There were only a few dozen pictures left now, ranging in quality from the moderately decent to the embarrassing; the rest he had either got rid of to a couple of clients, unloaded onto dealers, or decided to keep for himself. This last batch, in a fit of impatience, he had decided to sell at an auction and, as none was particularly valuable, he had arranged for them to go into a sale in London; they were not subject to any export restrictions and would get a better price there. They were, however, subject to a monumental amount of paperwork, which he had been sweating over for months. It was nearly all done now, most of the pictures were safely boxed and ready to go, but there still remained an alarming number of forms to fill in.

So he didn't blame Flavia for being alarmed; the Italian state in one of its full-blown moods of cranky irrationality is an alarming thing. But she had a sort of absentminded calm about her, which was really quite unwise.

It was not ingratitude that made Flavia dismiss Jonathan's counsel with a touch of impatience, she was merely preoccupied. Since being summoned to the prime minister's office, she had been totally consumed with the Claude while also having to put on an air of not having a care in the world. A long, early-morning phone call with the prime minister to try and extract more specific instructions produced nothing except a convoluted statement that gave the impression that he was unaware of anything to do with ransoms; after it was over, Flavia convinced herself that the call had been taped and would be used in evidence against her if need be. That started her day off badly, but even worse was the lack of any movement; the kidnapper did not follow up with any more details about how much money he wanted or how it was to be paid. Assuming a ransom was what he wanted. Time was short, after all; Flavia found the desultory approach quite surprising. Even the dimmest thief—and this character clearly was not dim—must realize that the longer he waited, the greater the risk of something going wrong, and that if the news came out, the price would go down dramatically.

At least the delay gave her time to do something, even though she had no great hopes of anything useful resulting. She could not send anyone out to ask questions, but she could comb through the records to see if any obvious candidates presented themselves. Again, she was hampered by not being able to tell anybody what she wanted, but fortunately the department had been assigned another trainee, who was, for once, unusually bright and keen. He had, she told him sternly when he came in, spent far too much time on the streets recently.

The trainee's face fell so far Flavia thought she might have to help him pick it off the floor. "It's all very well rushing about in flashy cars kicking people's doors down, Corrado, and don't think I'm criticizing. You kick them down very well. But the essence of policing these days is intelligence. Forward planning. That sort of thing. Very interesting," she added encouragingly. "So I've constructed a little exercise for you."

"An exercise?" Corrado, the trainee, said in a scarcely concealed tone of disgust. "You mean, not even a real case?"

"It might be one day. Got your notebook? Good. Take this down. Let's see now. Armed robbery at a museum. Lone operator. Painting stolen."

"What painting?"

"Doesn't matter what painting," she said. "It never does in real life either."

"Oh."

"Ransom demand. Pay up or else. Right?"

Corrado nodded.

"Good. Now assume this has all just happened. It's your job to head into the records and construct a list of potential people who might have been involved. Do you know how to do that?"

"Start with the computer, then go to the files, look for possibles for the theft itself, compare that with lists of people who are thought to have done kidnappings, etcetera." He sounded bored and annoyed. Flavia felt slightly sorry for him, but even if she had just told him a pack of lies at least one part was true. Sitting on your rear end reading files really was now the stuff of policing.

"Quite," she said brightly. "And I know you are going to grumble and moan about it. So the sooner you are done, and done properly, the sooner you can get back to the outside world. Off you go," she concluded in her best schoolmistressy tone, giving him an encouraging smile as he sloped out of her office.

That was all very well, and even cheered her up a bit, but the improving mood went into a sharp reverse shortly after she had finished her midmorning sandwich. As she brushed the crumbs carefully from her blotting pad into the wastepaper bin, her secretary—it was amazing how quickly you can get used to having a secretary—announced that a journalist was on the phone from *Il Mattino*. Common enough, quite a few checked in regularly to see if there was anything going on, and Flavia was very much pleasanter to them than Bottando had ever been. Ettore Dossoni was a new one to her, however; she vaguely knew the name, but he had never, as far as she was aware, had anything to do with art or theft before.

"I was thinking," he said in a tone that had just a touch of insinuation about it, "about writing a story on security."

"Oh yes."

"Yes. You know. Museums. Especially when pictures move around."

"You mean for exhibitions, things like that?" Flavia asked dryly.

"Just that sort of thing. You know. Look at insurance, the way they are guarded, what *might* happen if anything went wrong and a picture was lost . . ."

"Very good idea," Flavia said encouragingly. "Although I can't give you chapter and verse on anything. We haven't lost one that way for ages . . ."

"Of course not," Dossoni said in an oily fashion. Flavia was beginning to dislike him. "But you must have plans about what you'd do if something like that happened."

"We run around and try to find it," Flavia said. "Same as usual. No story in that."

"But if there was a ransom, say."

"Paying ransoms," Flavia pointed out severely, "is against the law."

"You mean you wouldn't pay one?"

"Me? Me personally? How could I? That's not my department. All I would do in those circumstances is pass on the request to a higher authority. As quickly as possible, I might add, although if you quoted me on that I would strangle you. Your guess is as good as mine about how they'd react. As I say, it's against the law."

She got him off the phone as soon as possible, then leaned back in her chair, a worried frown on her brow. He was clearly fishing. Someone had said something, but not enough for him to know what to do with it. Three possible sources: someone from the museum, someone from the prime minister's office, or someone involved in the theft itself. Not much point speculating about which. She picked up the phone and talked to some contacts about having the journalist's phone tapped. Ten minutes later, she had the response.

No.

That was the trouble with being new at the job. She had no clout yet. No one would have refused Bottando. Although, come to think of it, no one had ever refused her before either. It put her in a bad mood that lay simmering inside her until Argyll once more proferred his well-meaning, and quite possibly sound, advice.

While she was thus employed, Argyll was left at home, feeling terribly left out, abandoned, and slighted. On the whole he hit it off well with Flavia's work; he and it had cohabited nicely for years and tolerated each other with only a few hiccups along the way. He endured the frequent absences, the preoccupations, and the occasional flashes of ill-humor that the work generated in her, and her work, in return, had provided him with a fairly constant diet of entertainment. He had even, so he prided himself and Flavia readily acknowledged, given material assistance on a few occasions. The three-way relationship had become a little more complex when the great promotion arrived, not least because Flavia spent more time on the drudgery of policing and less time looking for stolen works of art. She had also become more like Bottando in office, more prone to calculate risks, see dangers, and watch for hidden traps. This occasionally gave her a furtive, not to say suspicious, air, and Argyll was interested to note that Bottando, relieved of his position, had become more like her—full of bright, if not always respectable, ideas.

He had been prepared for this and usually it was only an occasional problem. With this particular case, however, domestic life became all but unendurable in a matter of hours. Information had to be wrung out of her, her usual good humor had vanished, she would not discuss, as she habitually did, even the outlines of what was going on. Quite apart from the fact that she was, in his opinion, taking an appallingly silly risk in having anything to do with the case. The fact that it was her job and that she had been brought in by the prime minister seemed insufficient reason, in his opinion, for not ducking and diving for all she was worth.

So, while he waited for his wife to recover her equilbrium, he lay on the sofa, considering which of his own tasks he should tackle first. This thought process used up a great deal of time that the more censorious might have considered better spent on actually doing one of the tasks, but Argyll was particular and wanted to get the decision right. So his mind wandered from topic to topic. Papers. Export regulations. The weekly shopping. Back again.

And then he had an idea for Bottando's farewell present. He and Flavia would, of course, get him a conventional trinket of some sort to mark the occasion, but Argyll felt like producing something special. He liked the general, and Bottando liked him. He felt he'd miss the old fellow almost as much as Flavia would. And his idea for a gift was perfect. Not long ago they'd been to Bottando's apartment for a drink—the first time Argyll had ever been there, as Bottando rarely invited guests. A dingy place it was, too; Bottando's bachelor existence had never included much housework.

His apartment was where he slept, took showers, and kept his clothes, little more. They'd only been there for twenty minutes before going out to a restaurant nearby.

All the more remarkable, then, to see the little picture above the long-unused fireplace, covering up the old stained wallpaper. It was the only object in the entire apartment, in fact, that wasn't strictly utilitarian; Bottando had spent much of his career recovering paintings, but he never seemed to have wanted actually to have any himself.

But this one was lovely: oil on panel, eighteen inches by eleven, somewhat bashed and battered, and a representation of the Virgin with a baby flying around in the air just above her head. Unorthodox. Quirky. Not your average Virgin, in fact. Her face was uncommonly pretty, and the painter had added two extra characters on their knees before her, praying devoutly. It was nice, in decent condition, and an asset to any mantelpiece. Little sign of heavy-handed restoration, though the inevitable bit of touching up was visible here and there. Jonathan guessed 1480s or thereabouts and central Italian in origin, although the picture was so far out of his usual area of operation he was incapable of being more precise.

"What's this?" he'd asked, standing as close as possible.

Bottando had paused, and looked. "Oh, that," he said with a faint smile. "It was a present, given to me long ago."

"Lucky you. What is it?"

"I've no idea. Nothing special in itself, I think."

"Where does it come from?"

Another shrug.

"May I . . . ?" Argyll said, taking it off the wall before Bottando could say no, I'd rather you didn't . . .

He'd looked more closely and had seen that the damage and wear and tear were more obvious. Flaking in one part, scratches in another, but not bad nevertheless. Then he'd turned it over. No useful scribbles, just a little piece of paper stuck on, with a little stamp that looked like a house, and a number—382—written in faded ink. Not one that Argyll knew. He'd shrugged, put it back, and later jotted down the mark in a notebook he kept for these things; it was one of his rare shows of organization. Useful things, owners' marks; the only decent dictionary of them had been published three quarters of a century previously and was so out of date and incomplete it was only occasionally helpful. Argyll had the vague notion that one day he might publish a supplement, and ensure his everlasting fame. "Is it in Argyll?" people would ask in decades to come. Or they would, if he ever got around to doing it.

And now, nine months later, the picture and the mark came back to him. That could be his present. He could track down its provenance. Figure out what it was, where it had come from, who had owned it. Make all the details up into a little report. A gesture, nothing more than that, but a nice thing to have, he thought. Personal. Individual. Better than the little print or watercolor the office collection would probably produce.

The iconographies were of little help, but a start. Virgins with air-borne babies were generally taken to be an early representation of the Immaculate Conception, long before the doctrine took over the hearts and minds of the religiously inclined. The two figures kneeling before her probably had the faces of the donors, but might well also represent Mary's parents. And if it was an Immaculate Conception, then it had probably been painted for the Franciscans, who were early enthusiasts for the idea of Mary being born without sin. But he had no artist or even school to start with—just a guess at date and region. All he had was his note of the little stamp on the back. Great oaks from little acorns grow. Argyll phoned his old employer, Edward Byrnes, who said he'd ask around. He always said this, and rarely did anything about it.

This time it was different; within an hour Byrnes sent him a fax about an offer from a colleague for one of the pictures in Argyll's sale, saying that in his opinion the price was good and should be accepted, and added at the bottom of his note that he had tracked down the little house mark.

"According to those people old enough to remember, it certainly refers to Robert Stonehouse, who formed a collection of some worth between the wars. This was broken up in the 1960s; I have looked through the catalog of the sale for you, but the obvious match won't take you much farther. It is given as 'Florentine school, late fifteenth century,' although considering how wayward these people can be sometimes on attributions it could be by Picasso. It sold for ninety-five pounds so we can assume that no one in London at the time rated it. Stonehouse's villa in Tuscany went to some American university; they might know more."

Another hour with the reference books, books of memoirs, and other impedimenta of the trade brought some more details about the collection—enough at least to indicate that Byrnes's description of the collection as being "of some worth" was a trifle cool. It had, in fact, been a very good collection indeed. A standard story, such as he knew it; Granddad Stonehouse had made the money in jute or some such, son Stonehouse came over artistic and retired to a magnificent villa in Italy, from which vantage point he not only bought his pictures but also kept a canny eye on the stock market, being one of the few to do very handsomely out of the great crash of 1929—a calamity which caused art prices the world over to collapse, much to the delight of those collectors who hung on to their money.

The great and traditional cycle was completed in the third generation with the last Robert Stonehouse, who had his father's expensive tastes but lacked his grandfather's attention to financial detail. The result was the breakup of the collection, the dispersal of all those works of art to museums around the world, and the sale of the villa to the American university, which established some form of summer camp in the building that had once echoed to the voices of the leading literary and artistic figures of Europe.

So far, so ordinary, and there was nothing in the tale that might help. The point that tickled Argyll's interest was that the second Stonehouse, by repute, had seen himself as an artist-collector whose accumulations were not merely an assorted lumping together of high-quality bric-à-brac, but an artistic ensemble in their own right, every painting and tapestry and bronze and sculpture and majolica and print and drawing carefully acquired to form a perfect and complete harmony. An obscure achievement, certainly, one that virtually no one could ever appreciate, but a remarkable accomplishment nonetheless. A tragedy, in its way, that the whole thing was dispersed, but that was the point. In its way, Argyll thought loftily as he poured himself another drink and put his feet up on the sofa to contemplate his inspiration; collecting was the original performance art, transitory, fleeting, and evanescent. Called into existence for one brief moment, then blown away on the winds of change as economics had their corrosive effect.

And theft. Seen in that way, theft could be presented as an aesthetic act, part of the never-ending process of breaking up and reforming groups of pictures. Good heavens, he thought, I might even write my paper on this. Bottando's little gift and the conference taken care of in one fell swoop. Kill two birds with one Stonehouse, so to speak. Windy, no doubt, insubstantial and vague, perhaps, but just the sort of thing that goes down well at conferences. Besides, time was running short. He really had to get on with it soon, and he had no other ideas at all.

His labors didn't fill in any details about the little Virgin, however, although the research gave him hope. If the picture had caught the eye of Stonehouse, there might be something to it; merely mentioning its provenance should add a fair amount to its value if Bottando ever wanted to sell it. Provenance hunting is a compulsive hobby in its own right, and once started it is difficult to stop. There is always the temptation to see if you can push the picture's known history just a little bit farther into the past. Argyll had got back firmly to 1966 and had pinned down only one previous owner. He still knew very little and in any case the idea for the paper had tickled his fancy. And Flavia was so preoccupied and grumpy that he would hardly be missed if he went off to Tuscany to investigate. Better to keep out of the way for a few days.

He thought about, then got the number of the American university occupying the Stonehouse villa from directory inquiries, and rang them up. Charming people. Of course they had papers about Stonehouse; of course he could see them; of course they would be happy to put him up for a night if needed. Would that it was always so simple. Half an hour later he was packing his bag to be ready for an early train to Florence—and then on to the Tuscan countryside—the next morning.

5

Corrado, the trainee, had done an exemplary job. Not only had he unearthed almost everyone in Italy ever involved in art theft, correlated them with those people known to have a penchant for art, then constructed another list of those connected with organized crime, and broken it down by region (on the reasonable ground that most criminals are remarkably lazy and don't like commuting), but he had also typed his report up in two dozen typefaces, illustrated it with handsome (if largely meaningless) tables, and bound it into a properly professional-looking document some forty-five pages long, complete with references to the case files. Flavia tried not to look impressed.

"Very pretty," she said as dryly as she could manage, tossing it onto her desk. "Now, if you would summarize your findings?"

"None," he said with commendable directness.

"None at all?"

"No one in the files has the profile you need. That is, I was looking for people who work singly and have stolen something similar. I even broadened the search and assumed that the person who stole the painting might be acting for someone else, but still no one fits very well. I didn't manage to check everything, of course, but . . ."

Good, she thought. So he was fallible after all. A chance to be censorious. "Why not? Thoroughness is essential in these matters, you know. Without it . . ."

"Not all the files were there," he interrupted, cutting the ground away from her just as she was getting into her stride. "A few were missing."

Flavia ground her teeth. The sloppiness of some people was one of the few things that really annoyed her, largely because she had once been the department's worst offender in this regard. As a sign of her Damascene conversion, her ascent to the realm of responsibility, so to speak, her first act on moving into Bottando's office had been to issue a severe memorandum to everyone about signing out files, putting them back afterward and not resting coffee cups on them. Her second act had been to clear out all the old files from her office and send them back to the stacks.

The edict had as much effect as Bottando's similarly worded commands had had on her. Great gaps continued to appear, files were placed in the wrong year or the wrong category even on the rare occasion they were put back at all, and every now and then a bellow of rage would echo through the building's corridors as someone found a blank space where the answer to all their problems should have rested.

"That's your afternoon's entertainment sorted out then," she said. "You'd better find them. They must be somewhere in the building."

"Maybe. One isn't, though."

"How do you know?"

"The librarian said it's down at the EUR. General Bottando borrowed it yesterday."

"Do without it, then, but find the rest." She had ruined his day, she knew that. The poor crestfallen lad had hoped the splendid job he had done would have won her permission for him to get back to accompanying Paolo on his rounds.

"The faster you find the files, the faster you get out again," she added as he left the office. Then she leaned back in her seat. Really, she must get something for the nausea. The only reason she didn't was her certainty that the doctor would find something wrong. The word ulcer hovered in the back of her mind; the sine qua non of all good bureaucrats. She couldn't stand the idea. Then the phone rang. The ransom demand had shown up. And about time too.

It was classic stuff; so traditional that it caused a mental eyebrow to waggle up and down in suspicion. A telephone call to the museum—although it seemed that the poor robber had had a hard time getting anyone to listen to him initially—then a code word to demonstrate his authenticity. Chocolates, the man had said. Fair enough; only someone who knew about the theft knew about the chocolates. Then the demand: three million dollars' worth of mixed European currencies—how much simpler the Euro will make life for everybody in the ransom business—and a statement that the handover would be communicated tomorrow.

"I think you should come down here, by the way," Macchioli said after he had relayed this information.

"Why? There's nothing else is there?"

"Only this package."

"What package?"

"The one a deliveryman has just deposited in my office. I had to sign for it on your behalf."

Flavia shook her head. "What are you talking about?"

"It arrived five minutes ago. A courier. Don't know where it comes from. It's addressed to you, care of the museum."

"Why would anyone send me a package there?"

A silence from the other end.

"Very well, I'll come and collect it. While I'm on the way, could you see if you can remember anything else about the phone conversation. And get the tapes for me to listen to."

"What tapes?"

"We sent someone round, remember? Just in case you had a phone call. Connected tape recorders to the phone system? Didn't they?"

"Oh. That." Macchioli sounded doubtful. A small bead of apprehensive sweat put in an appearance at the top of Flavia's skull.

And rightly, too. For the technicians who fitted the equipment had done their job perfectly in all respects, except for trusting the switchboard operator of the museum to switch the tapes on every morning. She had put it on the first day, the vastly obese woman explained, more angrily than was warranted in the circumstances, but the tape kept running out. What was she supposed to do? Didn't people realize how tiring and stressful it was, answering phone calls all day and every day, without having to worry about changing tapes as well? It wasn't as if she was paid very much, after all. How often, she asked rhetorically, how often had she told her supervisor that they needed at least two people a day on the switchboard? But did anyone ever listen to her . . .

Flavia found she wasn't listening either, and she smiled politely at the indignant woman in front of her, and went back to Macchioli's office.

"No tape?" he asked.

"No."

He smiled apologetically. Flavia resisted the temptation to throw something at him. "You've remembered nothing else?"

"No. Except that we found the frame."

"Where?"

"In the conservator's office. What with all the excitement, we quite forgot we'd taken it out of the frame to give it a dust."

"I see. I suppose I'd better tell the prime minister about the ransom demand."

"Oh, I've already done that."

"When?"

"When the call came in."

"And that was?"

Macchioli looked at his watch. "My, how time flies," he said. "A couple of hours ago."

There was no point in mentioning that Flavia took it as a personal insult that she came so far down everybody's list of priorities. Macchioli would, no doubt, have inquired what difference it made. And, of course, it didn't make any difference at all.

"Splendid," she said. "Splendid. Now, this parcel. Where is it?"

Macchioli pointed to a large brown-paper-wrapped box in the corner. Flavia eyed it suspiciously. No one had ever sent her a bomb before, but there was always a first time. And, she supposed, a last time as well. On the other hand, why on earth would anyone send it here? She picked it up—it was surprisingly heavy, like a box of books—gave it a tentative shake, then shrugged and borrowed Macchioli's scissors.

Inside was money. A lot of money. A huge amount of money. A gigantic amount of money. She shut the lid rapidly. How much? It wasn't exactly hard to guess that there would be, in mixed denominations, precisely three million dollars. Nor that it had materialized as a result of Macchioli's call to the prime minister's office.

"Good heavens," the director said, as he came across and peered over her shoulder. "What's that?" He specialized in redundant questions.

"Well," Flavia explained, "it was my birthday a few days ago." She stood and picked up the box. "Do you think you could have my car come into the courtyard at the back? I would hate to lose this. By the way, what's the story of Cephalus and Procris?"

"Pardon?"

"The Claude. The subject?"

"Ah. It's Ovid, I think, although it was mainly known in the seventeenth century from the play by Niccolò da Correggio. Terribly complicated. The gods making mischief, as usual. Diana gives Cephalus a magic spear that never misses its mark; he aims at what he thinks is a deer in the forest and kills Procris by mistake. Then Diana brings her back to life again and everything ends happily. Why do you ask?"

"Curiosity. I've never heard of it."

"Really?" said Macchioli in surprise. "Now, when I was young, it used to be part of the school curriculum."

"What was?"

"Mythology. Everybody had it dinned into them. Mussolini was terribly keen on it, I believe."

"I suppose that all changed in the sixties."

"I suppose," Macchioli said, clearly not thinking it was a change for the better. "Shows your age, though. I imagine everyone over forty knows it quite well."

"In that case," said Flavia, "I'll stop looking for young thieves. Except that I don't imagine the subject mattered to him much."

6

The Rome to Florence bit was easy enough; simply a matter of going to the station, getting on the train, and staring at the countryside becoming ever more beautiful as the hours rolled by. An empty train as well, but not what it had been. Argyll was getting old enough to feel nostalgic on the slightest pretext, and the replacement of the ancient green wagons, which had once lumbered along stuffed with redundant conscripts, with shiny, new, fast, and expensive supertrains offering the dubious delights of airline comfort made him sigh for a simpler age.

On the other hand, it was a much faster way of getting there; he hardly had time to read the newspaper before the train slowed down and pulled into Florence. Then the simpler age came back with a vengeance. Whatever innovations modernity has brought in its wake, they have, as yet, had little impact on the Florentine bus system, which, though frighteningly thorough, is also incomprehensible to all except long-term residents.

So Argyll spent the next forty-five minutes shuttling among the dozens of stops outside the station in the hope that one driver would eventually admit to going in the right direction. Even when this hurdle was surmounted, all was not yet complete: the bus dropped him deep in the countryside at the junction of one small road, and another even smaller, with no signposts and no one to ask. He was left to admire the freshness of the country in spring, before the terrible Tuscan summer has parched the landscape.

Simply being out of Rome was a remarkable tonic; he loved Rome dearly, but there was no denying that it could be a touch smelly on occasion. And you only noticed the noise when it wasn't there any longer, when all there was to hear was the lightest of breezes in the tall cypress trees and the sound of those few birds that had not yet been shot and eaten.

Very agreeable—but he couldn't stand breathing in the fresh country air all day. He had a choice of two routes: to walk on along the road the bus had traveled, or to go down the little road to the right. Instinct told him to take the little path, so as was his wont he chose the other, on the grounds that his instincts in these matters were invariably wrong. Then, bag in hand and beginning to overheat, he trudged along for half a mile with not a house or a person in sight, until he paused to get his breath. It was only spring but it was already warm, and he was English. Anything more than tepid weather and he began to melt.

Silly to go back, daft to go forward. No phone. He cast about for inspiration, but there was none within reach, so he trudged around a corner and instead found salvation in the unlikely form of a man in a full three-piece pinstripe suit staring quizzically at an old Volkswagen with the front hood up.

"Excuse me . . ." said Argyll, in Italian.

"Damnable thing," said this man in English, paying him no attention at all.

"Pardon?"

"Damn car. Damn people. D'ye see? Someone's stolen the engine. Stop for a minute, come back, and it's gone. No wonder it doesn't go."

Argyll looked in. True enough. No engine. "Isn't it in the back?" he asked.

"What?"

"The back. That's where they usually are."

The man, a tall, ramrod straight individual with gray wispy hair and a look of astonishment on his face, gave up staring into the empty luggage compartment and turned to Argyll properly. "You a mechanic?"

"No. But if you don't believe me, have a look."

Now ever more perplexed, he did as he was told, marched around to the back and lifted the rear compartment. "Good lor'," he said. "How extraordinary. Well, well."

Then he turned back to Argyll. "How lucky of me to come across a mechanic. Perhaps you would be so kind as to get it going for me?"

"I'm not a mechanic."

"You clearly have a way with these things, though."

"Well, hardly . . ."

"Off you go, then."

So Argyll did what he always did with recalcitrant cars, that is make sure there was petrol, then tug every wire to see if any was loose. None was, but he must have done something, as the machine obligingly cemented his reputation as a wonder-worker by starting the first time he tried. His newfound companion was openmouthed with admiration.

"I won't ask how you did that," the man said. "I wouldn't understand, anyway. But my thanks, nonetheless."

Argyll looked modest about his expertise. "Perhaps in return you could do me a small favor," he said. "Do you know a place called the Villa Buonaterra?"

The slightest of hesitations, and the smallest look of doubt crept across the older man's face. "Yes," he said. "I do. Why do you ask?"

"I'm meant to be going there. But I can't find it. The bus driver said he'd drop me off at the nearest stop, but I don't know whether he did or not."

"Two hundred meters, on the left." He turned away abruptly, got into the little car, and drove off without so much as a word of thanks. Then stopped, reversed back to his original place, and wound down the window.

"Ungracious," he said sternly. "Always a fault of mine. Come and have a drink this evening, if you are free. A mile farther on. My little cottage. Just before the village."

Then he drove off again. Argyll watched him go, feeling that it was one invitation he would probably be willing to pass up.

Had the man also mentioned that, although a mere hop to the entrance gate, it was a mile farther down the drive to the house itself, Argyll would at least have been prepared. As it was, it took another half hour before he arrived, tired and dusty, at one of the most comfortably handsome bits of Renaissance architecture whose doorbell it had ever been his privilege to ring.

As he waited for an answer, he stood under the entrance portico between the columns of crumbling ocher stucco, grateful for the cool of the shade. Stretching before him was the gravel driveway, lined with lichen-covered statues, to the side the formal garden, laid out Italian-style, geometrical and disciplined, but with none of the severity and bleakness that the French version introduced later. Beyond were the trees, and he could just hear the slightest rustling of the leaves in the light breeze. *Buonaterra,* good land, indeed. If he had a lot of money, he would also live in a place like this, and fill it with the loveliest things he could find. A huge amount of money, rather: back in the 1920s when Stonehouse was buying, he was competing against only a few odd museums and a handful of eccentrics like himself prepared to lay out good money on fifteenth-century Madonnas and the like. Now the competition was Internet billionaires and multinational corporations. He didn't know how many items of the Stonehouse collection, which once hung on these walls, were now hidden away in darkened bank vaults, but he suspected it was probably a fair proportion.

So now the pictures were owned by the moneymen, and the villa, once the country hideaway of the Florentine nobility, was overrun by students playing with their Frisbees on the lawns. Progress with a price.

His air of melancholy peacefulness was just getting into its stride when the door opened and the soft accents of the American South brought him back to the new millennium. Half an hour later he had unpacked his bags, washed, and wandered back down to find his newfound Southern friend who had made it all possible.

"How many students do you have here?" he asked curiously, gazing around at what, to all intents and purposes, resembled a deserted country house, decorated with fine furniture, with not a trace of the institutional about it. He had imagined the wafting smell of boiled cabbage, the walls washed down in battleship gray, and the distinct signs of overuse everywhere. Nothing of the like to be seen.

"Virtually none," replied his host, whose name was James Kershaw. "I don't know why it is, but the chance of several months lounging in the Tuscan countryside doesn't seem to carry much appeal to our students. Although I suspect that the faculty who come every year do their best to discourage anyone from trying it. The whole operation," he continued, leading the way onto the terrace at the rear, which was laid out for lunch, "seems to have been lost down some administrative black hole. The villa was bought with a donation and can't be sold again, thanks to the eccentricity of the donor. The Italian department has shrunk in recent years and we insist that no one comes without speaking Italian. So apart from a few graduate students, we only get half a dozen a year. And they've not come yet."

"So the rest of the year you live like Renaissance gentry."

"That's it. Someone will notice and put a stop to it eventually, but I intend to enjoy it as much as possible while it lasts. Champagne?" he asked, before adding: "Not real champagne, of course.

If eight people got through a case of champagne a week, we might draw attention to ourselves."

Argyll agreed that restraint was perhaps wise in the circumstances.

"I'm pleased to see you. It's pleasant to have some company in our exile here. What do you want, exactly?"

"I have to write a paper. It's got to be done in a couple of weeks, and I want to use the Stonehouse collection as the central point of it all. And I want to look for a picture that used to be here. You did buy all his papers when you took this place over?"

"Oh yes. No one else wanted them. Twentieth-century collecting was not a hot topic among the art historical fraternity then. Still isn't. I don't recall anyone ever looking at them. What's the picture you're after?"

"A Madonna. I think it's a form of Immaculate Conception."

"By?"

"By the Master of the Buonaterra Immaculate Conception. That is, I don't know."

"And you want to find out. Are you a dealer?"

A loaded question. Confessing to being a dealer in academic circles is about as respectable as confessing to having academic interests at a gathering of dealers. You get nods of understanding, and brave smiles, but the air of disdain that enters the conversation is quite unmistakable. Neither entirely sympathizes with the other, as the scholars consider dealers to be interested only in money, while dealers hold that the academics are vague and inefficient. It is generally quite the other way around, but no matter. Argyll was instinctively reluctant to confess his shameful past, and so babbled instead.

"You think it's a lost masterpeice by Giotto? Is that it?"

"No, no. It's only a detail. It's the paper that's important. A sort of philosophic ramble on the art collection as a work of art, looking at how collections and dispersals have their own aesthetic form. You know. Start with Sulla looting Athens for Rome, Constantine stealing large portions of Rome to take to Byzantium, then on to the Venetians looting Byzantium, Napoleon looting Venice, the Germans looting Paris. Then conclude with the breakups of collections after the war for tax purposes and it all going to America. All looking at how it disseminates styles and enhances the value of certain works. That sort of thing."

Kershaw, whose own scholarly works had titles like "Gender and Intertextuality in Late Venetian Fresco," sniffed. "It's what you do with the material, I suppose," he said doubtfully.

"Quite," replied Argyll stubbornly. "And I don't have any material at the moment, which is why I'm here. So if you will lead me to it, I will set to work."

"Finish your lunch first. We normally have coffee on the balcony, then get back to work properly rested. Do you want to eat this evening as well?"

"Probably. I've been invited for a drink by some old buffer whose car I got started. English fellow, by the sound, and some sort of retired soldier, by the look. And a bit loopy, I think, so I don't imagine I'll be there for long."

"Old Volkswagen?"

"That's the one. Who is he?"

"Robert Stonehouse."

Argyll raised an eyebrow.

"He had to sell up here, but has a very nice little place a mile or so down the road. He's had to give up the opulent lifestyle, of course, but still has more money than you or I will ever see in our lives. He's not very fond of us. Did he invite you for a drink before or after he knew where you were going?"

"After."

Kershaw looked impressed. "He must have taken to you, then.

Normally even mentioning this place is enough to put him into a bad humor. He's never quite accepted his fall. On the other hand, if you want to know about this picture, he will be the man to ask. Probably far better than reading any papers. If he was around at the time."

7

The moment she knew that Bottando had been sniffing around in the files after talking to her about the case, Flavia remembered that dreamy look in his eyes, and knew that he was about to pull his "we old men may be past it, but you'll find that experience does have its uses" routine on her. Normally she would have humored him, waited until he got around to pulling off his little coup, dropping in with a look of satisfaction on his face and presenting—*voilà*—his suggestions. And she would have looked terribly impressed and grateful.

But she was in a bit of a hurry, and this particular business was not good for her patience or sense of dramatic flair. So she rang him up instead.

"File," she said. "The one you took. What's it about?"

Instead of the tone of smug self-satisfaction she'd been expecting, however, Bottando sounded rather upset to hear from her.

"And there was I hoping to surprise you," he said. "Dear me. I must be losing my touch. If you would like to join me for lunch, I will tell you what occurred to me. It may be nothing, of course, but it might give you something to occupy your mind a little."

Lunch was the last thing she wanted, her stomach was still so iffy, but she knew that Bottando was quite dedicated to the business of maintaining civilization in this particular form, so she agreed. Salad and water she could probably deal with.

"It was the chocolates that did it, of course," Bottando remarked forty-five minutes later when they had settled, ordered, and crunched their way through a couple of breadsticks. "How old are you, my dear?"

Flavia scowled. It was going to be one of his long, urbane performances. Oh well. If he produced the goods, it would be worthwhile putting up with a bit of smugness.

"Thirty-six," she said.

"Good heavens," Bottando said. "Are you really? Well, well. How remarkable. Forgive me for asking. It is none of my business, I know, but are you and Jonathan ever . . ."

Flavia scowled some more. Sometimes, the ability of Bottando to sound like her mother was almost eerie. Besides, the ticking of the clock had begun to sound rather loud of late.

"You're quite right," she interrupted tartly. "None of your business."

Bottando harrumphed. "And not to the point either," he said hurriedly. "All I wanted to know was how well you remember the late seventies."

It was going to be a long one. "Well enough, I think. Why?"

"Maurizio Sabbatini. Ring a bell?"

"No."

Bottando looked faintly pleased. "No reason why he should. He was never of any great importance. Didn't come to trial even, so his name wasn't well known. However, he was very much a member of the extreme left back then, and committed to direct action to bring down world capitalism. You remember the sort of thing, no doubt."

Flavia nodded patiently. The food arrived. Bottando tasted, and ate with appreciation. She picked.

"You are going to continue, I hope?" she prompted after a while.

"Of course, of course," Bottando replied, wiping a touch of truffle juice from his mouth. "October 1979—I have read the file, you see, hence my precision at dates—he robs a bank in Turin. Solo effort, it seems, he never believed in working with other people. A frightening, and then bizarre, experience for all concerned. He wears a face mask, waves a gun at people, collects the money. Then he throws it all out of the window, recites a poem about the coming revolution, and hands out chocolates all around. Takes a bow, and leaves."

Bottando paused as the plates were taken away, the glasses refilled.

"Chocolates," Flavia said.

"And face masks. One of the pope, this time. He had always had a sense of humor, it seems, even as an urban guerrilla. And although nominally classed as a terrorist, he was only ever on the fringes of the really dangerous groups. He knew them all, of course, but found their high seriousness and dedication tedious. They, in return, considered him too whimsical and unreliable to be trusted.

"Anyway, such stunts were hardly the sort of thing which meant he could remain unidentified for long. But he was never brought to trial."

"Fancy that."

"Indeed. The file is silent on the matter."

"And then he becomes an art thief with a weakness for the seventeenth-century Italianate landscape?"

"No. He becomes an artist. A performance artist." The air of faint disdain was easily detectable. As far as Bottando was concerned, the only good thing to be said for any art after about 1850 was that it was a blessing when it was stolen.

"He isn't particularly successful, as his particular brand of heavy-handed social critique is a bit out of tune with our cynical age. He's regarded, indeed, as rather quaint, and quite possibly gets gallery space out of nostalgia rather than for any serious admiration for what he does. Most of the people handing out the money, after all, are of the same generation. That's how it appears, anyway. There is, I suppose, a certain kudos to be had in patronizing a terrorist, even one who is a bit long in the tooth.

"There we are. He only has a file with us for cross-referencing purposes, so it's not complete. But it does indicate a tendency toward whimsical parodies of crime, the chocolates, daft face masks, and a habit of working alone. Combine that with a career going nowhere and the possibility of raising large sums of money."

Flavia thought. That Bottando had produced the goods was almost certain. But she was annoyed he'd sat on the information.

He did, at least, have the grace to look sheepish.

"Now, what I was going to do was tie it all up for you, and present him on a plate. My swan song. I didn't intend to take the credit, you understand. Just have a final fling before retirement. Unfortunately . . ."

"Oh no."

"Possibly a good thing. I was contacted by the prime minister's office, and told that I was to take charge of this personally. I did protest on your behalf, but they were quite adamant on the matter."

Flavia scowled. Even she noticed she was scowling a lot these days.

"I also mentioned that I—we—could quite possibly recover the painting without paying any ransom, given a moderate bit of good fortune. But I was very firmly told to do nothing of the sort, as you were as well. Pay the money, get the picture back, and forget it. It was made clear that any attempts to prosecute would probably be squashed in that devious way that the state has sometimes. I imagine that the reasoning is that there could be no trial without publicity. And publicity is just what they want to avoid."

"Hmm."

"Hmm is as good a reaction as any," Bottando commented.

"I assume that this man Sabbatini has vanished?"

"Of course. You'd hardly expect him to be at home."

Flavia shook her head in disbelief. "You really could have told me all this . . ."

Bottando looked properly shamefaced. "Of course I should have. You're quite right, my dear. Quite right. I should have. But has it made any difference?"

She paused. "I suppose not. It's just that I always seem to be the last to know anything these days." She tried, but failed, to make her objection sound as though it was more than mere pique.

"So now we have to bring this thing to a conclusion. Which means we need the money, and some routine for swapping it."

She sighed heavily, and told him about her morning.

"You have three million dollars in a suitcase in your office?"

"In the safe. And it's in a cardboard box, not a suitcase."

"Whose money is it?"

"How should I know? Someone close to the prime minister, obviously. Apart from that, I've not a clue."

"Any arrangements made for the swap?"

"In the next couple of days."

"I'd better do that, I think."

Flavia began to protest.

"Orders, Flavia, orders. And probably better in any case. If something goes wrong, I get blamed, not you. I think Friday would be best."

"Why Friday?"

"Because my retirement starts officially on Friday. Caution, you know. Too late to take my rather reduced pension away, even if it is a complete fiasco."

8

While all this was going on, Argyll was doing his best to live the life of a country gentleman, absorbing the quiet and peaceful atmosphere of the Tuscan countryside at its most beautiful.

Then he reluctantly puttered into the muniments room, where the superefficient librarian had already got out the Stonehouse dossiers for him and put them on a table by the open doors, and sat down to read.

He did quite well, in the circumstances, these being the growing warmth of the air, the lazy buzzing of the early bees, and the chirruping of the birds as they flew around making their nests in preparation for the summer of endeavor that lay ahead. It would have been so much easier to sit back in his chair and watch them at it, to have let his mind drift while he monitored the thin wispy clouds passing in a leisurely fashion across the sky.

And in truth he did a fair amount of that; several of the clouds received more attention than they strictly deserved. But he did at least drag his mind away for long enough to make a dent in the dreary buff-colored files that lay in front of him. Long enough, indeed, to garner everything he needed for his paper, thanks to the librarian and her photocopying machine. While she was busy, he turned his attention to searching for information on the little painting of the Virgin.

A painting of the Immaculate Conception: late fifteenth century, oil on wood, with no previous history; it simply popped into visibility as an indeterminate Madonna in 1940 when Stonehouse bought it in London after he'd fled back there at the start of the war. Not even the name of a dealer to help out. There was nothing odd about that: only a privileged few paintings can be traced back very far, and the reluctance of auctioneers to help out makes matters worse. Stonehouse bought it for forty guineas; hardly vast riches, even for the period.

He then took it back to his villa in Tuscany, had it cleaned—a bill for 125 lire was attached—and hung it in a bedroom on the second floor where it stayed until it was moved to London and put up for sale with most of the other Stonehouse pictures in 1966. This, according to the papers, was something of a scandal, which was good; there is nothing like a bit of naughtiness for putting up value. The newspaper clippings demonstrated the impact the auction had made; not because the sale was so valuable but because the collection was the biggest example of wholesale smuggling in recent Italian history.

To take a painting out of the country without permission was one thing; to take 124 of them without so much as a by-your-leave was quite another. The younger Stonehouse had maintained (rightly) that nearly all the pictures had been bought in London in the first place and he was merely taking them home. The Italians maintained (also rightly) that they were still Italian pictures and export permission was required. Sorting it all out took six months and a vast amount of correspondence, none of which, fortunately, was necessary for Argyll's case.

Unfortunately, it seemed ever more likely that the picture, however old, was no great masterpiece. He was disappointed, but not surprised. In the listing of the Stonehouse collection the attribution was the same as the one in the auction catalog, and the picture hadn't even been on general display; rather, it had been consigned to a lesser bedroom where it had as company a pastel portrait of the collector's grandmother by one of the more unmemorable Scottish painters of the Edwardian era on its left and a French revolutionary print depicting the execution of Marie Antoinette on its right. What could you make of that? Did Stonehouse see granny as a cross between the Virgin Mary and the Queen of France?

There was one simple and obvious answer. Go and have a short walk in the park and a nap for the rest of the afternoon before drinks with Stonehouse Junior. Then a good night's sleep, and back home the next day. One of the rare advantages of art history is that, when you do find yourself with time on your hands, you are often in an excellent position to make the most of it. There have to be some compensations for the salary, after all.

This plan he followed without deviation, apart from briefly postponing his nap by five minutes to phone Flavia, failing to reach her. Thus, at six o'clock sharp, he was to be found walking slowly up the path to Robert Stonehouse's cottage. Or what Stonehouse called a cottage. He may have come down in the world, but not to the level occupied by most of mankind; the house was still impressively large, with a huge and opulently decorated entrance hall, the black-and-white–patterned marble of the floor already doing its job of damping down the heat of the day and rendering the interior pleasantly cool.

Stonehouse was all hospitality and apology, both for his incivility of the morning and for his inability to offer him anything more than a drink or two.

"I do not cook myself," he said with no regret at all. "I know I should and that it demonstrates how I live in the past. It is just that I find the past a more pleasant place. I would rather live there with bread and cheese than in the present by a stove."

"You must eat more than that."

"Five days a week someone from the village comes to look after me. Today is not one of her days. She is old, unfortunately. If she dies on me I will be faced with a choice. Modern life or starvation. Which do you think is best?"

Argyll, who rather prided himself on his skills with pot and pan—largely without justification, although his abilities were superior to those of his wife—acknowledged that it was a difficult choice, but suggested that some people found that cooking gave considerable pleasure. Stonehouse was not convinced.

"Wear a pinny, have your fingers smelling of garlic or fish? No; I see the pleasure in eating, just as there is delight in the appreciation of art. But the idea that cooks, or painters for that matter, are anything but vulgar artisans I find unacceptable. Have you ever met a pleasant, intelligent painter? One you would be happy to have in your house? Of course not."

"I imagine you must have been brought up with painters in the house."

"Good heavens, no. My father once made the mistake of inviting that Modigliani fellow, but threw him out. Damn man tried to seduce my mother. That was before I was born, of course."

"Very bad manners," Argyll agreed.

"And wanted to be paid for the portrait," the old man continued, the indignation still in his voice.

"You have a portrait by Modigliani? Of your mother?"

"Certainly not. My father took it into the garden and burnt it. No great loss."

"Well . . ." Argyll said, trying to remember how much the last Modigliani to be sold had fetched.

"There's more to life than money, Mr Argyll. How do you think I would have felt knowing there was a painting of my mother with no clothes on in some American museum?"

"I see your point."

There was a lot to be asked here, Argyll thought. Like, what was his mother doing taking her clothes off in the first place? On the other hand, it might have been considered tactless to mention it.

"It was very kind of you to invite me this evening," he said, swerving on to what he hoped would be a less complicated topic. "I wanted to ask you about a painting in your collection; I've spent the day going through the archives at Buonaterra but they didn't have anything I needed."

Stonehouse considered becoming indignant at the mention of his old house, but decided against it. "Oblige if I can," he said.

"An Immaculate Conception."

Stonehouse furrowed his brow.

"Little thing," Argyll continued hopefully. "On panel. Florentine, maybe. Didn't fetch much at the auction. Used to hang in a bedroom. Called a Madonna, then. The Immaculate Conception bit is my guess."

"Oh yes," he said. "That one. I remember now. The one that got stolen."

Argyll's heart lurched as it always did when the words "painting" and "stolen" appeared too closely together, then slotted back into its normal position. After all, it wasn't his picture.

"Very odd business," Stonehouse was saying.

Argyll forced his mind to pay attention. "Ah."

"Can't tell you the details. I only arrived at the last moment, so much of what I say is secondhand. As I understand it, someone noticed one morning that it had gone. My father called the police, they found it and brought it back. End of story, really."

"Who stole it?"

"They never found out. Or, at least, no one said. Someone obviously knew more than they were letting on."

"What makes you think that?"

"Because they said they found it in a ditch about half a mile away from the house. The story was that the burglar had stolen it, then panicked and thrown it away when he discovered it wasn't the painting he wanted. Or some such."

"And what was wrong with that?"

"It was a painting on wood. Quite resilient on one side, relatively speaking, but very porous on the back. And it had been raining. There would have been at least some damage. In fact there was none at all. My father reckoned that it had been kept indoors throughout its absence. But we didn't bother to inquire. After all, we'd got it back speedily and if we'd made a fuss the insurance company might have taken too much interest and put up the premiums. Besides, I think my father knew who had stolen it."

"Really?"

"Or at least, who had wanted it stolen. Ever heard of Ettore Finzi?"

Argyll shook his head. Stonehouse chuckled. "You have just made my father very happy in his grave, young man. Finzi was my father's greatest rival for this sort of picture. It was a battle that lasted over thirty years. Whenever it was heard my father was going to bid for a painting, Finzi would turn up as well, even if it meant traveling to London from his house in Rome for the purpose. Their rivalry bid prices up quite unnecessarily. Finzi hated my father, and my father, in return, came to have a complete detestation for Finzi, because of his behavior."

"Just the rivalry of collectors?"

"Oh no. A complete clash of personalities. They were different in every way. Inherited money and a life of ease on my father's side, self-made man on the other. Different background, different upbringing, different nationality, different attitude to art in every respect. Finzi wanted his collection to batter his way into the establishment. Whereas my father considered it a triumph to pay as little as possible, Finzi was most pleased when he spent as much as possible. Entirely different, you see."

"And this painting? Why would he want it?"

"According to the story, which my father used to tell perhaps too loudly to make Finzi seem ridiculous, because he couldn't change a car tire."

"Pardon?"

"Whenever it was. The dealer where my father bought it. I don't know who heard about the picture first, but there was a dash through the streets to the dealer. My father got there first as Finzi's Rolls-Royce had a puncture and he didn't know how to change a tire. So he had to walk the last half mile and by the time he arrived, my father had bought the picture for a bargain price. And insisted that Finzi admire it in the street when he arrived, all breathless and flustered. Within a few days everyone in Rome had heard the story, and Finzi never forgave him. My father told me the story when the picture was stolen."

"This was nineteen forty?" Argyll asked.

"Nineteen thirty-eight, I believe."

"Are you sure it wasn't later?"

"Oh no. It came from a dealer in Rome, I'm sure of that. My father left Italy in late 1939. Finzi smuggled himself out later."

"Why?"

Stonehouse looked puzzled, then remembered he'd missed out a bit of the story. "He was Jewish. And realized he had better make a dash for it. I don't know how he managed it but he arrived very hard up, apparently. My father lent him money to tide him over, although that didn't heal the rift between them in artistic matters. Hostilities were resumed on that front the moment hostilities ended on the other."

"And the picture was stolen . . . ?"

"Nineteen sixty-two."

"That's a long time to harbor a grudge."

"Not for a man like Finzi," Stonehouse said. "He vowed that one day he would have that picture, and knew that time was running out. He was old and ill—in fact, he died the following year. So he was in a hurry."

"But there was never any evidence."

"Oh no. But then it didn't matter. He didn't get it and he was

IAIN PEARS

ill. Why persecute him in his last months? Although I suspect that knowing my father couldn't even be bothered to take any action was the last straw for him. It might well have been that last show of disdain that tipped him into his grave."

A paper on the psychology of collecting? Argyll thought. The rivalry that drives men—always men, how many women collectors have there been in history?—to such extremes that they will steal from each other to possess the things they want. A bit of connoisseurship, bit of Freud, bit of history? Maybe.

"But who actually stole the picture?"

Stonehouse looked uninterested. "I've no idea. I wasn't there, alas. The only people in the house were my father, a young student who'd taken his fancy, and a few of his fellow connoisseurs. Most of whom are now dead, I imagine, except Bulovius, who is still on this earth—although not for much longer. Must be ninety if he's a day."

The good old days indeed. Argyll had heard of Tancred Bulovius, one of those hybrid collector-scholars who no longer exists in any great number. One of the more opinionated connoisseurs in his heyday, which was properly the late 1940s and 1950s. Probably a detestable man, but encyclopedic in his knowledge, the representative of a time when scholars might properly hope to collect the works of art they wrote about, publish only when they had something to say, and stay as guests for weeks on end at the country houses whose archives they were using. Changed days. Argyll, for a fleeting, nostalgic moment, could grasp Stonehouse's objection to the modern world.

"I've never met him."

"You should hurry if you want to. He won't be around much longer. Can't say I ever liked him. He didn't know what to do with the young, except deliver monologues at them. But it may be that he's mellowed since he hit ninety. At least he must have given up chasing after everything female that comes within four miles of him."

"I didn't know that was part of his reputation."

"Oh, Lord, yes. Quite incorrigible he was. Not a man to take no for an answer. The poor student who was here eventually fled the house, he was such a pest. Poor girl. Pity; she was a pretty young thing. And recently married, as well, if I remember rightly. Not that details like that ever stopped Bulovius. You seem remarkably interested in this, if I may say so."

"A friend now owns the picture," Argyll said. "So when I found your father's mark on the back, I thought I'd find out about it for him. I take it he's not in possession of stolen goods?"

"No, no. It was recovered, as I say. And then sold along with everything else."

"I'd like to know more about the theft. Spicy details like that always add a little cachet to a picture."

Stonehouse considered this. "I can't help you. The only people who might would be this young girl . . ."

"Name?"

"Can't remember. She was only here for a few days. Mainly lived in Poggio di Amoretta. That's a village near here. Close to where you must have got off the bus, in fact. Then there's the investigating magistrate . . ."

"Name?" Argyll said hopefully.

"Ah, now, I remember that. His name was Balesto. I remember him because I read that he died about six months ago. I'm now at the age when I find obituary columns quite fascinating."

"Ah."

"Bulovius, of course. He's still alive. Just."

"What about the policeman?"

Stonehouse squinted at him, his head held to one side. "Policeman," he said. "Can't say I paid too much attention to him. Let's see now." He made a Herculean effort to remember the trivialities of the people he had met.

"No. Can't remember," he said. "There were two of 'em. One

old, fat, and stupid. Trying to ingratiate himself. Wanted to be invited for dinner, I think. The other was young, gangling, and had hair that was much too long. I remember wondering how he got away with it."

"And the names? I don't suppose you remember either of them?"

Another shake of the head. "No. However, I believe you will find it in my father's papers at Buonaterra. This man kindly gave some advice about protecting the villa and wrote it all down for my father to send to the insurance company. Look in there, and you'll probably come across it. And there'll be the report on the theft there as well."

Argyll had reached a dead end, and knew it. So he turned the discussion on to Stonehouse's father, his collection, what it was like being brought up in a Tuscan villa after the war—better than an English school, it seemed, although he sort of knew that already—all the sorts of subjects Stonehouse loved talking about.

He left an hour and two bottles later, and wove his way back to his bed. He had rather enjoyed himself.

The next day, Argyll went back to Rome, but only after reading the insurance file and the police report it contained. A summary only, little more than the initial deposition by Stonehouse and an account of the picture being found. He also discovered from the files that the policeman who had recovered the painting was a youthful, inexperienced, tall, gangling, long-haired Taddeo Bottando.

9

"ong-haired and gangling?" Flavia gurgled. "There aren't any
Lphotographs, are there?"

"I'm afraid not. But it must have been his first brush with art,
more or less."

"Heavens. I must ask him about it."

"So must I. It would fill in a few details about that picture."

Flavia, he noted, was a wife transformed. Enthusiastic embrace,
beaming smile, everything a weary husband could want on his
return home after a voyage. He was most surprised.

"Action at last," she said. "It was sitting around all the time that
was getting to me. And this damnable stomach of mine."

"No better?"

"Not really. But not at all important. The thing is, this evening
I hand over the money, and get the picture back. Then I can get to
work properly."

"So? Tell me."

"Midnight. Down the Appian Way. Very dramatic. Just me,
although Bottando has offered to drive. Very exciting."

"Too exciting. Don't you think it's a bit dangerous?"

She shrugged. "Not really. Not if he wants the money. And he
works alone, and has no reputation for violence."

"I thought you said he was a terrorist."

"Not a real terrorist. I mean, he uses guns that play Verdi."

"What if he has one that doesn't play Verdi?"

Flavia shrugged.

"Flavia, I'm serious."

"So am I. I want to get this over and done with. I can't take any-one else because they'll figure out what's going on and talk. I can't delay it, even if there were any point in delaying. Don't worry, Jonathan. Bottando will protect me. He knows what he's doing."

"He's sixty-five," Argyll pointed out. "And horribly overweight. Not much use, in my opinion. What would he do in case of trouble? Roll on them? Please let me come with you."

"No."

"Flavia . . ."

"No. Absolutely not. If you must worry, do it here." She picked up her coat. "I won't be long," she said as she opened the front door. "Promise."

"You see," she said brightly four hours later as she bounced through the door. "I told you."

Considering that they had been four of the longest hours of Argyll's life, this was almost too much. He had not only not slept—it was now nearly two in the morning—he had paced. And groaned. And imagined all sorts of terrible things.

"You could have phoned."

Flavia looked upset. "Sorry," she said. "I should have. I forgot." Then she peered at Argyll. "Oh, Jonathan. Have you been wor-rying?" And she gave him a big apologetic hug to make matters better.

"Well, I don't know about that . . . ," Argyll huffed.

"Don't you want to hear what happened?"

"I suppose," he said, determined not to give way either easily or gracefully.

"It was a triumph . . ."

"Hmm."

"A vast success."

Argyll sniffed haughtily.

"And a textbook example of how to do it. Almost."

Argyll glared at her, then relented. "Oh, very well, then," he said crossly, and threw himself on the sofa. "Go on."

Flavia took off her coat and sat cozily beside him. Then stood up again and poured herself a large glass of whiskey, and then went to get some water for it. She liked ice in it, too, but refrained for fear of damaging Argyll's sensibilities. It was good whiskey, after all.

"I picked up Bottando," she began eventually, "and off we went, and arrived about ten minutes early. The Mausoleum of Herodias, do you know it?"

Argyll nodded.

"Big, round, middle of a field. No other cars around that I could see, so he must have trekked across the fields to get there."

She took a sip. "Then we had a fight."

"Who?"

"Me and Bottando. He pulled rank on me. And appealed to my sense of fair play."

"You're an Italian. You don't have a sense of fair play."

"Yes I do. Anyway, he started by saying, poor little woman, it's much too dangerous. A bit like you. And I told him to get lost. Then he said that he was still my boss, so he was ordering me to let him do the swap, and I told him to get lost again. Then he pointed out that this was his last ever official act as a policeman that was going to be worth anything."

"Good point," said Argyll.

"So I let him do it."

"And?"

"And that's it. He waddled off into the darkness with a case of money, and waddled back ten minutes later with a Claude Lorrain. Unscratched, untouched. The man had been there, hiding behind some rubble, they had a brief conversation, and it was all very businesslike. No danger at all. A pleasure to do business with, in Bottando's opinion. A man of his word, Signor Sabbatini."

"How do you know it was him?"

Flavia shrugged. "I don't. He was wearing the regulation ski mask, Bottando said. But what he could see fitted his description. Frankly, I don't really care at the moment. We've got the picture back. National scandal averted."

"You are sure of that?"

"Oh yes," she said with a smile at his ability to worry. "I'd told Macchioli in advance and we went straight to the museum. He'd been pacing up and down as much as you, I think. He was a complete wreck by the time we arrived. He examined it very carefully and was satisfied. Not a copy slipped in in the hope we wouldn't notice or anything like that. The ultraviolet markings on the back were all still there, canvas repaired in the right places, and so on."

"So he's happy."

"Delirious. As was the prime minister. Well, delirious is not perhaps the word. But he did say thank you. Which is something. The only blot on the horizon is that I am under official instruction to lay off Sabbatini."

"Why?"

She shrugged. "Because there is nothing we can do to him without revealing that we had that picture stolen from underneath our noses. And that, the powers that be consider, is more important than putting him behind bars."

"So he's got away with it? Lucky fellow. Or clever."

"Isn't he. However," she went on, "there is nothing to say I can't make his life as miserable as possible. And if he so much as commits a parking offense, I'll pull his head off."

She smiled happily at the prospect.

"I suppose," Argyll said. "And my congratulations. Now for the really important business. Did you talk to Bottando?

"What about?"

"That picture. The Immaculate Conception. Did you ask who gave it to him?"

Flavia looked puzzled. "Oh, that," she said eventually. "Sorry. I forgot. My mind was on other things. I'll do it next time I see him. Now, can we go to bed? I'm so tired I feel I'm about to die . . ."

For the next few days, life returned almost to normal—or not, in fact, because it was so quiet and peaceful. Argyll delivered his last lecture, began his vacation, and came close to starting serious work on his putative paper. Flavia was equally underemployed as the thieves, burglars, and other criminals of Italy had momentarily, it seemed, run out of inspiration and enthusiasm for their job. Apart from routine events easily handled by others, there was little to stop her from organizing her desk, flitting about the departmental corridors of power making useful contacts and doing a little quiet lobbying for more money.

She was still not confirmed in her post, however. That was the only cloud in an otherwise delightful spring. But she managed to put it to the back of her mind, somehow. There was little she could do about it.

And she never got around to asking Bottando about his picture, for while she sat at her desk waiting for something to happen and Argyll idled away the days, the general cleared his papers, filled out the forms, and with surprisingly little emotion or display, slipped away from the life he had led for thirty years or more. A long holiday, richly deserved, he said. Somewhere quiet.

She was disappointed. Pleased, of course, that he had so few regrets, but slightly upset as well. Was this what happened eventually? Would she, in due course, be so fed up that she could walk away from job, friends, colleagues, and life without even a moment of regret? Besides, she had always thought she had a special rapport with her old boss. Fine that he didn't miss anyone else; but she wished he regretted parting company with her. He could have said good-bye properly, rather than with just a phone call.

It was the only moment of discomfort in an otherwise quiet interlude, enjoyable because she knew it wouldn't last long. Sooner or later it would come to an end. And it did, sooner rather than later. A small cloud on the horizon to begin with, no bigger than a man's hand, but the harbinger of violent storms.

Performance artist found dead in his own exhibit. A small headline in the paper, and a report that found a place because the whole country was consumed with the same somnolence and because it allowed the journalist concerned to give free range to his slightly tasteless sense of humor.

Maurizio Sabbatini had, it seemed, managed to drown himself in a vat of plaster he was sitting in during the creation of a work of art entitled *Pompeii Revisited*. Taking his cue from the casts of corpses made by archaeologists who dug up the Roman town, his show was a commentary (the program said) on death, and the coldness of a science that converts tragedy into museum exhibits. Sabbatini plunged naked into liquid plaster and sat there in the gallery that hosted his concept. Visitors passed through to see him staring blankly into space, sleeping or singing mournful Neapolitan songs to no one in particular, and were supposed to reflect on the transience of life, the permanence of art, and the discomfort of bathtubs.

Or not; the trouble was that the audience reaction was too undirected, according to another practitioner who quietly opined that it was Sabbatini's great weakness—fatal weakness, as it turned out—as an artist. His performances were so vague that no one was ever sure what he was on about. So, when he mixed too much plaster into water, sank underneath in a drunken stupor (another weakness of his), and drowned as it set hard around him, none of the small audience passing through thought it at all odd. Indeed, no one noticed he was still there for days, by which time the embarrassment in the gallery was considerable, and the mirth of the journalist all but uncontrollable. The only thing that alerted them, he reported, evidently shaking with so much merriment he could scarcely type, was the fact that Sabbatini did not replenish the trademark supply of chocolates he always left around for visitors to eat. When someone—in fact a cleaning lady—did finally notice and the authorities were called, he had to be excavated with a pneumatic drill, at which point the journalist writing the story became so incoherent with mirth that he was unable to give basic details such as when the great artist had actually died.

Only after she had read the report twice, with some twitchings of self-righteous pleasure herself at the clear demonstration of divine vengeance, did Flavia realize that lying around somewhere might well be a great deal of money and that she'd better get a move on before someone noticed it. Not that she didn't trust her colleagues, of course, but she didn't want to have to give explanations if she could avoid it.

The happy thing about corpses is that it is so much easier to search their possessions; no question of infringing their rights or anything like that. Treading on the toes of colleagues is much trickier, the more so if you cannot explain what it is that you wish to investigate; the affair of the Claude was, after all, still under wraps. Flavia, however, was long practiced in fobbing people off with vague statements about leads and general lines of inquiry, sugaring the pill with promises of full explanations later. Nevertheless, it took a full morning to do the groundwork, and it was well past lunchtime when she decided to take Corrado, the trainee, with her, for educational purposes.

"You remember that hypothetical case I gave you a few weeks back?" she asked, as the car drove them across the city. "It wasn't hypothetical."

"I did wonder," the oversophisticated young man replied.

"No. Real painting, real theft. And a real thief. We're going to visit his apartment."

"Will he be there?"

Flavia explained something of the circumstances. Corrado displayed a degree of restraint lacking in all others who had heard of it so far. "Poor man," he said. "What was the picture?"

"That is the one thing that remains classified."

"That important?"

"No comment. It doesn't matter, anyway. I got it back."

This produced genuine admiration and surprise, which Flavia, though she tried to resist, rather enjoyed.

"Now, this man. What we will be looking for is the usual sort of thing, I imagine. Notes, diaries, phone bills, anything like that. He was once upon a time involved in the hard left, so I imagine he'd be too experienced to provide us with anything, but you never know your luck. He must have been as poor as a church mouse. He seems to have lived hand-to-mouth for the past couple of decades; sitting in bathfuls of plaster can't have been that lucrative."

At which comment the car drew up outside one of the most expensive apartment blocks in the Parioli district. Flavia avoided the trainee's look of skepticism at her deductive powers.

"Are you sure we're at the right address?" she asked the driver crossly.

" 'Course I am" came the less than respectful reply. She didn't mind; he talked like that to everyone. Always had.

The apartment in which the mouselike, poverty-stricken, anti-materialist former revolutionary lived was even more opulent. Extremely modern, but filled with the most expensive furniture and paintings—even what looked like a real Chagall. Closer inspection revealed wardrobes full of clothes from the most prized designers, a refrigerator stuffed with enough champagne to inebriate most of the world's terrorists at a sitting, and floors covered with exquisite silk Persian carpets.

"More lucrative than it seems, perhaps," Corrado said quietly. "How much was the ransom?"

"Who said anything about a ransom?"

"Oh. Sorry . . . I assumed . . ."

She shook her head. "No, you're quite right. But he can't have bought this with the ransom." She didn't bother him with the details of how she was so sure.

"Maybe he made a habit of it?"

She stood looking at an autographed Warhol soup can, feeling bewildered, then laughed. "A fine example, young man," she said, "of the dangers of jumping to conclusions. Let this be a lesson to you."

He grinned back, acknowledging her grace in admitting having made a slight fool of herself. It was the sort of openness that had already won her a following in the department. It was hard to replace Bottando and be anything but his successor, but she was making more progress than she realized.

"Right," she said, feeling better already. "Go through his drawers, find any papers, and any photographs. I'll go and knock on a few neighbors' doors and see if I can get a handle on this man."

What you need in such circumstances is someone who thoroughly disliked the man you are investigating. Faced with questions from the police about people you like, there is a natural tendency to be vague, even among the wealthy of Rome, a group that perhaps has less sense of fellowship with the rest of mankind than any other on the planet. The phrase "Oh, I wouldn't know anything about that" to avoid saying something impolite about a neighbor has derailed many an otherwise promising investigation. Neighborly tension, on the other hand, is a great loosener of tongues.

Alas, Sabbatini was not prone to play his music loudly at two in the morning; did not trade drugs in the corridors; did not leave his rubbish out on the wrong days; did nothing, in fact, to suggest he was anything other than a quiet, respectful member of the Roman *haute bourgeoisie*.

And that was exactly what he was. Flavia discovered his dark secret after five fruitless interviews, conscious all the while that nearly all the information she needed was almost certainly in the complete dossiers she had not yet been sent. Interviewee number six had a grudge of epic dimensions: the communal garage.

Far more than politics and religion, even more than noise and dirt and indecent behavior, laying claim to someone else's parking space is just the sort of thing to let the passions rip. And Sabbatini and Alessandra Marchese had, it seemed, been locked into such a struggle for more than six months. Every time he saw it free he parked his car in her space, even though he knew it was hers; even though his was free. He did it deliberately, she said, the outrage visibly rising in her face, her hands beginning to quiver with fury. It was appalling. She had complained to the building's management but they, of course, were hopeless. Just because he was well connected, they behaved like mice . . .

Flavia nodded sympathetically. The woman was detestably self-righteous and self-important, but a perfect treasure trove. "Perhaps you would tell me more . . . ?" she murmured.

Half an hour later she had it all. Some details no doubt exaggerated, some even invented, but a portrait of the man in the sort of detail only pure bile could generate. Signora Marchese noticed him in a way neighbors do not ordinarily pay attention to those who live around them. Indeed, every time she saw him, heard him, or even smelled his cologne in the elevator, she froze, and could think of nothing else for hours afterward.

She appeared to have spent much of her time shopping, so could not provide a perfect record, of course, but did remarkably well. Stripping out the rancor, Flavia emerged with a picture of a man who, apart from his penchant for vats of plaster and other people's parking spaces, lived a remarkably quiet, unflamboyant life. He did little, it seemed, rising late and apparently not working. Signora Marchese, who lived a similar existence, did not find this odd; Flavia wondered where the money came from. When asked, the signora shrugged and said, "Family." The universal explanation, which explained nothing.

He had few friends, few callers; no girlfriends, not even any boyfriends. He'd been away for over a week, although last Wednesday somebody—presumably he—had been in the apartment. She'd heard bumping and scraping as though someone had been rearranging the furniture. If he was an artist—and the signora seemed shocked by the idea, as if she had suspected him of terrible sins but not ones of that magnitude—then he did whatever he did somewhere else. All in all, the very model of a perfectly respectable member of the idle rich, whiling away his time, dabbling in this or that, spending lavishly on whatever took his fancy and doing no harm to anyone. But.

Corrado, meanwhile, had collected enough information to fill out more of the picture; a substantial monthly sum was paid into his bank account. A sheaf of letters from lawyers indicated that the law firm was where the regular payments came from. Splendid, but first things first. She sent Corrado off in a taxi to talk to the forensic brigade, and went to Sabbatini's studio herself.

Had she been truly concerned with looking good in the eyes of her subordinates, this would have been a mistake; it is always better to spend your time talking politely to the respectable than wandering around getting your hands dirty. And the studio—little more than a lock-up garage at the back of a run-down housing development, one of those thrown up twenty years ago without any building permit and built so shoddily they were now falling down again—was a very dirty place. Lots of plaster, execrable sculptures made of old tin cans and household rubbish, bad paintings on the walls, all the bric-à-brac of the talentless dabbler—for Sabbatini, she decided, was utterly without merit as an artist. One thing, however, was of vital importance, and justified the trip even though it did little but confirm what she already knew.

In a drawer in a desk was a cheap paperback copy of Ovid's *Metamorphoses*. Hardly conclusive, even Flavia realized that. But it was the origin of the story for the Claude, and was Sabbatini really the sort of person who would idle away his hours reading Ovid? Just as well he was dead and there was no chance of a prosecution, she thought. She could imagine the look on the investigating magistrate's face if she told him that the entire case rested on a myth. But it was enough to reassure herself that she was heading in the right direction, and to keep alive her hopes of getting back the money. She found it hard to suppress the idea that retrieving the money would do marvels for her chances of hanging on to her job.

She mentally wrote the report on the way back to the office, then listened to Corrado's account of the autopsy, his first, and something that he had not greatly enjoyed.

Nothing remarkable. Lots of alcohol, and death by drowning. No signs of foul play, but nothing to rule it out either.

She nodded absently as she munched through a ham sandwich and Corrado looked at her with distaste. "Time of death?" she asked. "I don't suppose they know, as usual?"

"Wednesday morning at the latest. Probably Tuesday evening."

She stopped eating. "What?"

He repeated himself. "Why do you looked so shocked?" he added.

She sent him off quickly. A trainee was the last person she was going to tell that not only had Sabbatini been dead before he collected the ransom, he'd probably even been dead before asking for one.

10

Trailing after Sabbatini wasn't, perhaps, quite so important if he hadn't actually stolen anything to start with, but Flavia had a dogged and thorough strain in her character that propelled her out of her office despite the discouragement and her growing conviction that her stomach was consumed with ulcers so vast in size that she might not survive them.

So she trudged wearily to the lawyers who had been channeling generous sums of money in Sabbatini's direction for so many years, and used her authority, her powers of persuasion, and best of all, her manifest ill-humor, to prize open their lips. And what she learned suddenly made her world terribly complicated again.

Maurizio Sabbatini was the brother-in-law of Guglio di Lanna.

"How very interesting" was her only comment. The lawyer made no response; it was a statement of the obvious.

She thought about it on the way back to the office, and at the same time felt a pang of regret that Bottando was no longer in place to give her his advice. Tangling with the Di Lanna family was the sort of thing that required all the help you could lay your hands on.

Not the richest family in Italy, certainly, but currently one of the most powerful, as the do-it-yourself political party that Di Lanna had forged out of the wreckage of the past few years of political chaos was now keeping the government in office. The Party for

Democratic Advance—no one knew what that meant, or even whether it was left wing or right wing—had only fourteen members in the Chamber of Deputies, but as the government as a whole had a majority of only twelve, its influence was far beyond its nominal strength.

On top of that, Di Lanna's tentacles stretched throughout Italian industry and finance; he owned nothing, controlled little, but through a whole series of investment groups and holding companies he had a stake in almost everything. He had mastered the art of making relatively little go a very long way. He was a powerful man, but with no power base; an illusionist who had vast influence because everyone thought he was influential.

And his brother-in-law was, it seemed, a terrorist who might, in his last days, have turned art thief.

Di Lanna was a deputy and she finally tracked him down in the most unlikely of places, the Chamber of Deputies itself. Except for set-piece occasions when the television cameras are switched on, members of the chamber, above all important ones, rarely turn up there, so to find a man of his stature in the office assigned to him as the leader of a party was all but astonishing. No secretary, no aides guarding the approaches, no noise and bustle of petitioners coming to and fro to indicate the presence of an important personage within. Just a little typed sign on the glass door, taped over a more permanent, painted one announcing that this had once been an office belonging to the now-defunct Christian Democrats. It was so quiet that Flavia scarcely expected to find anyone in; she bothered to knock only because it seemed silly to go away without trying.

But Di Lanna was not only there, he even opened the door himself, another all but unimaginable piece of behavior. Important people in Italian politics—in any politics, come to think of it—do not open doors themselves; it indicates they are not, perhaps, that important after all. Di Lanna seemed prepared to take the risk of

falling in people's estimation as he waved her into the cramped little space without ceremony. Man-of-the-people act to show his left-
wing credentials? Flavia thought. Or maybe a touch of American
informality to indicate his orientation toward business and free market economics? She shook her head. She really must make an effort
to keep it all simple.

"You're early," he said.

"Am I?" she replied, a little surprised.

"Yes. You're not due until four, I think. No matter. Let's get on
with it. Don't expect me to say anything interesting, though."

"I wouldn't dream of it," she said before she could stop herself.
To her surprise, Di Lanna threw back his head and laughed. "Sit
down, sit down. What's your name, by the way?"

He sat himself and looked at her carefully, a slightly impish air of
curiosity about him. Thinking about it later, Flavia decided it was
his eyes that made up her mind; no one not fundamentally sound,
she thought quite unreasonably, had eyes that twinkled in such a
mischievous fashion. Di Lanna was one of those people she instantly
liked. It took some time to figure out why he confused her, though.
He dressed a little tweedily, an old establishment indicator, aping
a supposed English style evoking images of land and country values. But everything else suggested the new left—the haircut, the
way of sitting, the hand movements. A deliberately confusing
onslaught of associations, which had the effect of always slightly
catching unawares those he talked to.

"Who do you think I am?"

"You're yet another journalist, aren't you? Come here to wonder
when I'm going to stab the prime minister in the back?"

She handed over her identity card. Di Lanna did not look surprised. "Might I ask," she went on, "if your office is entirely safe for
conversation?"

He paused for a second. "Every Wednesday morning, someone
places a bug or two in here; every Wednesday afternoon I have it

taken out again. They know this, but keep on doing it. It's to serve notice I'm under surveillance, not because they expect to hear anything of interest. At the moment, we should be quite safe."

"And who are they?"

He shrugged. "Whoever. The dark hand of the state. You know. Perhaps you should tell me why the art theft police is here to see me?"

She hesitated only a second. "Because you may be related to an art thief. As you know quite well, as I assume it was you who provided three million dollars for a ransom payment last week."

Di Lanna pouted in the sort of way that indicates that losing three million dollars is a matter of the utmost triviality. As, indeed, it probably was for him.

"Ah," he said. "I was told it would be handled discreetly. And that there would be no investigation. I must say, I am disappointed."

"You needn't be. All I am doing is tying up a few loose ends. The whole business has become a little more complicated since your brother-in-law's death."

She noticed that mentioning Sabbatini produced not even a conventional look of dismay or regret on the politician's face. If anything, there seemed to be a shadow of satisfaction on his closely controlled features.

"I would have thought it would have simplified things for you. That has been the effect on me."

"Quite the opposite, in my case," she replied. "It now seems that he was dead before the ransom was either asked for or collected. Which means that either he was working with someone else—who knows all about the whole embarrassing business and has the money—or someone was deliberately using his style of playacting to confuse us."

Di Lanna looked curious.

"I am presumably not the only person to know about your relationship to him," she went on. "We must consider the possibility that this whole stunt was aimed at you, rather than anything else."

He swung in his chair—another Americanism—then put his hands together, fingertips on his lips, priestly fashion. An old Christian Democrat habit. "Seems unlikely, surely? The only point to that would be if everyone knew about it. In that case—you're right—it would be damaging."

"My point is that it still might be. The money is out there, and someone knows the full story of the theft, the ransom, and—as he has the money—he also has the convincing evidence to prove it. I suspect there is little we can do; whoever this character is, he can't be touched without there being some risk of everybody discovering that the Italian state managed to lose a picture it promised to guard with its life. Nor that it, and you, connived in an illegal act to get it back again. Which, I assume, you do not wish to happen."

"Not really, no."

"So I shall be very careful. But I do think it is important to find out if possible who this other person is. Then there will be less chance of a nasty surprise one morning when you open the papers."

Di Lanna considered, then nodded. "Perhaps wise. I always knew that little shit would cause more trouble sooner or later."

"Might I ask what contact you had with him?"

"None whatsoever. I haven't seen or spoken to him in any way for nearly twenty years. As far as I was concerned, he didn't exist. He betrayed everyone he ever came into contact with."

"But you still gave him money."

Di Lanna looked inquiringly.

"I talked to the lawyer who paid him a monthly allowance."

"That was money from his father, held in trust. Had I been able to stop it entirely, I would have done so. I spent a fortune on legal bills to try and get him excluded, and largely succeeded. But I couldn't manage it all. What he was left with was enough to make me wonder why he did this when I heard about it. His one good quality—his only one, perhaps—was that he genuinely did not care a hoot about money. If he had it, he spent it. If he didn't have it, he didn't care."

"He seems to have changed his ways, then."

Di Lanna shrugged.

"Can you tell me anything about him? Friends, associates, that sort of thing?"

Di Lanna shook his head. "I think the voluminous police files would be more use. As I say, I refused even to talk to him."

"Was he that bad?"

"Yes. The damage he did was incalculable and unforgivable."

"He didn't do much, though. Apart from rob a bank."

"You are very forgiving for a member of the police, signora. However, I was not thinking of his politics, or his self-indulgent antics. I was referring to his murder of my wife. His sister."

Flavia paused to take stock. "I'm sorry," she said after a while. "I'm not with you."

"Maurizio fooled around with these people, and being him couldn't help bragging about his family connections—he was happy to play revolutionary, but never wanted it forgotten that he came from a rich and powerful family. Maybe it was his way of rebelling against his father, who was a formidable man. Very powerful, determined, and insistent on getting his own way. He doted on his daughter, and had no time for his son. I don't know, and I don't care.

"These people had no more loyalty to Maurizio than he had to them. For them he was a joker, a source of money, no more. And when they wanted to pull off a really big coup, they exploited him mercilessly. He told them all about his family and their houses. He told them all about his sister, what shops she liked, what restaurants she frequented. My wife, signora. I loved her more than anyone I have ever loved, before or since. We'd been married for eighteen months, that's all.

"The rest is simple, if painful. They took her, then made their demands. I got the money ready—I would have paid twice as much—but the police were unusually effective for once and found the house where they thought she was being held. There was a siege, which ended in shooting.

"It went terribly wrong. There were terrorists inside and they were all killed. But Maria was not there. And the response was immediate and savage. She was found the next day, dumped behind a bush in the Janiculum near a statue. She was twenty-four. They had shot her in the head. It killed her father, and nearly sent me mad with grief. May twenty-fifth, nineteen eighty-one. The day my life ended."

Flavia sat back in her chair and thought. She had no memory of the tragedy.

"No," he said. "It was one of the many things that were hushed up, as much as possible. It would have been an enormous propaganda coup for them and we felt that at the least we could deny them that. Her body was collected before the press could get there, and we put out the story she had died in a car crash. It pained me, not to have the reason for my loss known, so people would understand, but it was the right thing to do. I thought so then, and I still do."

He shrugged helplessly. The look of pain on his face was all too real and immediate. "I've never really got over it, I think. And I have certainly never forgiven him. So don't ask me about him now."

"I'm sorry. I didn't realize . . ."

"How could you?" He paused, and thought, swinging in his chair once more, but gently and without affectation this time. "Prime Minister Sabauda was interior minister at the time; he broke the news to me himself. Stayed with me, comforted me."

Di Lanna smiled, very slightly. "I am always asked when I am going to bring him down, pull out of the coalition, and try to increase my own power at his expense. The answer that I can never give is that I am not. I owe him gratitude for the way he helped me through those dark times. I can never say that, of course; my credibility as a politician, such as it is, would be destroyed if it became known that I was acting out of motives like loyalty and gratitude. So I have to talk about unity and stability instead. Which, of course, are taken to be code words for biding my time until I trip him up."

Flavia shook her head once more and felt a wave of nostalgia for nice simple criminals. You always—generally, at least—knew where you were with them.

"I see," she said. "I think. What do you think Sabbatini was up to, then?"

"I have no idea, and I don't care. The picture has been recovered, and happily he is dead. May he rot. Three million dollars is a small price to pay for that."

He reached over his desk and picked up a picture frame, which he handed to her. It was of a young woman, holding a bunch of white flowers, smiling at the camera. It had the look of distant history on it already.

"She was pretty," Flavia said, not knowing what else she could say.

"She was delightful. Everything I ever wanted. We never had any children, alas. That would have been some compensation, at least. He denied me even that."

"I'm sorry."

Di Lanna made an effort to bring himself back to the present.

"Why did you provide the money for the ransom?"

"Because the prime minister knew the moment he heard of the theft who had committed it, and when he told me I offered to help. One must take responsibility for members of one's family, however despicable they may be. Sabauda was very worried about using public funds; the chances of someone noticing would have been large. I assisted. That is all. As I say, for me it was a small thing financially. The emotional cost, you might say, was much higher."

Di Lanna looked at his watch. "Now, I'm afraid you must excuse me, signora . . . ," he said gently.

Flavia got to her feet. "Of course. I apologize. I have taken up far too much of your time already."

"What will you do now?"

"I will tiptoe delicately around the matter, and see if there is anything to be done to tidy things up."

"May I give you a word of advice? Leave it be. There is nothing to be gained from it. My wife was buried without explanation. Let Maurizio go the same way. He deserves no better.

"And," he added, showing for the first time the slightest flash of claw—not much, nothing overt, but nonetheless there and all the more impressive for it—"it will win you no thanks from anyone."

11

Try as he might, Argyll could not rid himself of the idea that there was something decidedly odd about Bottando's little Virgin, and the thought of it preyed on him mightily. It was not that it was urgent, that was certain, but it was a distraction and Argyll, when Flavia was occupied and there was, in theory, nothing to keep him from his work, loved distractions. He sought them out, in fact, finding almost any reason, good or bad, to avoid settling down, concentrating, and putting pen to paper. An almost physical itch came over him, and the need to jump up and go off and do something—check some detail, verify some fact—became overwhelming.

Bottando's picture was the perfect distraction. So perfect that even Argyll knew that his feeble attempts at resistance would be dismissed by the overwhelming, primary urge to delay, dither, and hesitate on the subject of the art collection as work of art.

In fact, he got down scarcely more than a sentence before giving way: "The study of collecting has a long history, but the collection itself has never, to my knowledge, been analyzed as an aesthetic object in its own right. In this paper I intend to . . ."

A good start, he thought to himself, leaning back and reading it over once more. Definite. Say what you mean, then get on with saying it. But, as with all good starts, it was important that the next sentence be just as effective. No letdown; no bathos. That would be disastrous. Suddenly grasping that such second sentences need to be crafted with precision, he threw down his pen, and decided that long reflection was required to get it just right. And he reflected best when walking. And he could justify walking only if he was doing something.

So why not just spend some time—only half an hour—having another little stab at the Virgin? Having thus convinced himself that stopping work entirely was by far the best way of getting his paper done, he brought his mind to bear on the problem of approaching the old Englishman Tancred Bulovius, perhaps the only person left alive who could tell him about the events at the Villa Buonaterra in 1962. He was not entirely enthusiastic, and, if writing his paper hadn't been the only alternative, he might well have recoiled from the prospect. There is something about the Grand Old Men of connoisseurship that, if not actually repellent, is at least a touch off-putting. Few are wholly agreeable; most have ideas of their own importance far in excess of the normal human tendency for self-aggrandizement. Many, in other words, are ticklish characters to deal with.

But there was no escape. It was Bulovius or hard graft. After many hesitations, he picked up the telephone and held his breath. An hour later, he was on his way to meet the last great Titan of Italian Renaissance studies. It would, no doubt, have been more polite to have waited, and to have made a proper appointment for the following day, or following week, but that would have given him time to write the paper. Besides, he reasoned, Bulovius was at least ninety-two. And with people like that you really can't afford to wait. Even an hour might make a difference. He could pop off at any moment. Also, the person who answered the phone seemed quite happy to have him come around.

How did these people manage it? he wondered as he arrived. Maybe it was just their age, their good fortune to have been born when sterling was a giant among currencies and modest means by English standards meant you could live *en grand seigneur* almost anywhere in Europe. Happy days, indeed, if you had the right passport, but those days were now long since gone. Even though he lived in it only a few months of the year, just after the war Bulovius had taken over the *piano nobile* of a sizable palazzo a stone's throw from the Piazza Navona. The city's notorious rent control saw to the rest. Unfair.

A palace is a palace, even if it clearly needs a bit of rewiring, the windows look as though they might fall out at any moment because of rot, the plumbing leaves more than a little to be desired, and the whole thing has the air of not having been lived in properly since Rome was ruled by a pope. You always have to make a choice between elegance and comfort; the Palazzo Agnello perhaps erred a little on the side of elegance, but in Argyll's opinion the sacrifices would have been worth it. Except in winter, when the lack of heating might have been a disadvantage.

In spring, late on a warm afternoon, few of these problems were obvious, except the fact that the old Roman aristocracy's distaste for fresh air meant that there were no balconies or terraces to sit out on. Turns the skin brown, makes you look common; no noble would have been seen dead looking anything other than pasty-white. Times change, palaces don't; Bulovius received Argyll in the grand salon, in semidarkness, and it was nearly ten minutes before his eyes adjusted fully to the gloom.

He could barely make out some of the renowned Bulovius collection hanging on the walls, and much of it wasn't that interesting; most had been spirited back to England over the years and now rested in Bulovius's house (less grand, more practical) in Queen Anne's Gate, where it awaited its owner's death: Bulovius had long ago done a deal with the British government for his collection to go to the National Gallery in exchange for a forgiving approach in the matter of death duties on the rest of his fortune. Argyll suspected from what he had heard over the years that the government probably wouldn't do so well out of the deal; Bulovius's fondness for money and for art were equal, and both matched his antipathy toward paying taxes of any sort.

Either way, it looked very much as though the National Gallery should be busying itself clearing out a room or two in preparation for receiving its legacy, for Bulovius did not seem long for this world. In fact, Argyll thought after he sat down opposite the old man, he looked as though he'd died several years ago. Not the picture of health: shriveled, gray, tiny, and hunched up in his chair, wrapped up despite the balmy afternoon heat in a thick tartan rug, with watery eyes and hands that shook uncontrollably. Argyll was surprised; it was not what he'd been expecting, and when Bulovius spoke he understood why.

"And how can I help you, young man?" Instead of a thin weedy voice to match, Bulovius positively boomed across the room at him, speaking with a firmness that was astonishing given his decrepit frame. Argyll paused before saying anything, uncertain whether he should speak according to what he saw, or what he heard. He decided it would be more polite to address the voice.

"Well," he said, "I wanted to ask . . ."

He got no farther. Bulovius shook his head, grimaced, then looked around him. "Is the door closed?"

Argyll said it was.

"Good. In the cupboard over there. Quickly. There's a bottle. Bring it to me."

Alarmed and convinced that without his medicine the old man would conk out on him and ruin his afternoon, Argyll leapt out of his chair and hurried across the room in the direction indicated. He could find no pills or potions.

Bulovius clicked his teeth in a clatter of impatience. "Whiskey, man. Whiskey. There must be a bottle there."

"No. Nothing."

"Damnable woman, she must have found it."

"Pardon?"

"My nurse. She keeps on confiscating it. Says it's bad for me. Of course it's bad for me. But, good heavens, what does that matter? Go to the kitchen. It must be there."

"What if she won't give it to me?"

"She should have gone out. Quickly, quickly. Bring yourself a glass as well."

Very doubtful about the wisdom of all this, but taking the old man's point about the futility of a keep-fit regime, Argyll walked in the direction indicated, and spent the next ten minutes wandering around the vast apartment looking for the kitchen, and even more time rummaging in kitchen cupboards looking for the bottle Bulovius so ardently wanted.

"Where have you been? I could have died of old age waiting for you," he said when Argyll finally got back. Argyll looked at him uncertainly. "A joke," he continued. "Don't worry. I can make them at my age. I'm ninety-three. Don't look it, do I?"

"Ah . . ."

"Of course I do. That's what you're thinking. And you're right. I could drop dead at any moment. Right in front of you. What would you do then, eh?"

"I don't know," Argyll said. "It's never happened before."

"I'd take that drawing, if I were you."

"Pardon?"

"That one. Very valuable." Bulovius pointed to a small sketch by the fireplace, in such a dark and dingy corner Argyll could barely see it. "You could grab it, walk out, and who'd ever know, eh? Go on. Take a look. What do you think?"

Oh, dear. Games. Argyll did hate them. The little examinations these old buffers like to set. It's no longer considered good behavior to ask who your parents are, what school you went to, never has been to ask how much money you have, but for some reason it is still acceptable to set these little tests. Can you spot a hand? Ascribe a subject? Argyll reluctantly heaved himself out of his chair, and took up the challenge.

If he was going to be tested, at least he would do it in better circumstances. Without asking, he took the drawing off the wall and carried it over to the window where he could see it properly. Nice frame, very old, but that meant nothing; the drawing itself was about four inches square in sepia ink, firm bold lines sketching out the torso of a man stretched in a muscular pose as if throwing something. The shading was equally effective, not a touch too much, with an economy of effort that was simply beautiful.

How do people recognize hands? Argyll, who spent much of his time and once derived much of his income from doing just that, was never sure; it is not something that can be put into words. Even the habitual patter of the connoisseur explains nothing, but merely describes an irrational feeling about a picture. It is by this person, or by that one, it is not a logical process of deduction; nothing to do with the intellect.

And in this case, Argyll was 99 percent certain he was looking at a sketch by Castiglione. Partly it was the pose, which reminded him of a painting he'd once seen in Ferrara; partly it was the line, which was also characteristic. Partly it was the ink, that brown shade like dried blood. But there was the final 1 percent of doubt that remained. What was it? Why did he hesitate to say? The drawing was perfect, beautiful and flawless. Was that the problem? Was it too much like Castiglione? Were there too many signposts? Did any painter, quickly sketching something for a larger work, reveal so much and unwittingly put so many signposts to himself in so few lines? Maybe they did; it is not a matter of reason which allows 1 percent of doubt to challenge 99 percent of certainty. Still less to outvote it.

"I think this is a wonderful, beautiful copy," he said, a little breathless from nervousness. He knew this was just a silly game but, having picked up the gauntlet, didn't want to drop it. "Studio of, apprentice to, that sort of thing. I'd guess the right period, even the right place, but not authentic."

It was part of the game, part of the bandying around of little signs, not to bother saying which artist he was talking about. That was taken for granted, he implied, only an amateur would bother even mentioning such an obvious detail. It was no more necessary than saying that it was a pen-and-ink sketch.

"If you suddenly dropped dead on me, I don't think I'd risk a visit from your vengeful ghost to take it. I'd rather have this." He gestured at a small and bedraggled oil sketch by the side of the window, propped up on a little stand on the bureau. "I've always liked Bamboccio."

He'd passed; his instincts had saved him once again. He could see it in the slightly disappointed look on Bulovius's face, the way the look of triumph had to be packed away for use at a later date. That's the trouble with the younger generation, the old man had looked forward to reassuring himself, no eye. Very skilled, no doubt, read all the *theorists,* but no eye, and without that, what's the point? Argyll, however, had read no theorists and had spent much of the last seven years doing little but looking.

From Bulovius he got no words of impressed approval, just the gruff comment, "Put it back where you got it, then. Don't hold it in the sun until it fades. Then come and tell me what you want." A sort of acceptance, Argyll supposed.

"Robert Stonehouse," he said, now he'd earned his audience. "Nineteen sixty-two. You visited him for a few weeks, I believe."

"If you say so," the old man replied. "It's a long time ago. Should I remember it?"

"While you were there, a painting was stolen. It vanished, then was recovered from a ditch. The person responsible was never found, nor does anyone seem to know why it was stolen. I want to know everything you can tell me about it."

99

He wasn't certain there'd be a great deal to say, but Argyll was a thorough person and he wanted everything he could lay his hands on. Not that it would lead to anything, but he still wanted to get it right. To his considerable astonishment, Bulovius remembered quite a lot. It just wasn't what he had expected to hear.

If it is possible to look perturbed, amused, and ill all at the same time, Bulovius came close. "What do you want? A confession? Very well, then," he continued before Argyll could assure him he wanted nothing of the sort, "I confess. What else do you need me to say?"

Argyll gaped at him, now thoroughly lost for words.

"It was stupid, I know. A moment of madness, brought on by irritation. I hope you realize that I have never, before or since, done anything like it. Every picture, bronze, print, and drawing that I own was acquired honestly. I have records and receipts for everything; what's more I must assure . . ."

"*You* stole it?" Argyll said, finally waking up to the fact that all his fond imaginings of the past few days had been completely wrong. Just as well he could still identify painters; he was obviously not cut out for anything more subtle.

"Yes, yes. I stole it. I can't even say I gave it back voluntarily; I suppose you know that already."

"Well . . . ," Argyll thought for a few seconds, trying to catch up with this unexpected slant on things. "Why did you steal it?"

"Because that barbarian Stonehouse didn't value it enough. He hadn't a clue what it was, the dolt; and the way he acquired it was despicable in the extreme."

"Why despicable? I heard he beat this Finzi man to the deal, but that's hardly despicable. All in the game, really."

Bulovius looked irritated. "What are you talking about?"

"I'm not sure anymore," Argyll said. "I heard that Stonehouse bought it in 1938 from a dealer in Rome. On the other hand, his own accounts suggest he bought it in 1940. . . . His son told me the 1938 version is correct."

"No, no, no. What nonsense. He's lying. Or more likely is just parroting what his father told him, as he always did. Finzi bought it; bought two panels out of a triptych from the dealer in Rome. Stonehouse would never have had the gumption to notice them. He never tracked down the third part. They must have been split up when they left the church of San Pietro Gattolia in Florence."

Argyll was disheartened to hear that he was now dealing with two pictures rather than one. He had hoped life was about to become simpler, not more complicated. But he smiled encouragingly.

"These two pictures . . . ?"

"Finzi, as you can imagine, had trouble getting out of Italy when things became dangerous. A lot of his fortune went in bribes and many of his pictures were given over then as well. He got some out, but arrived in London with almost no money. Stonehouse offered to lend him money, taking what pictures were left as security. After the war, when Finzi reestablished himself, Stonehouse refused to give them back, saying that they had been bought. It was a dreadful blow. The cream of his collection was dispersed and even though he built a new one, it was never quite the same. It was a deep personal wound, as I'm sure you can imagine."

"Not how Stonehouse tells it."

"Finzi was a natural. Loved paintings—had a better eye than anyone I ever knew, for all that he was a businessman. Everything he ever bought was a gem. And a kind man, as well; he took me on to order his collection when I was a penniless student in Rome, and paid me a salary until I got my first job. And made me the chief beneficiary of his will. Except for the pictures that went to the National Gallery."

Ah. Argyll thought. That's where it all came from.

"Stonehouse was loathsome; he never had to earn any money himself, so didn't know its value. Just its power. And he bought rubbish; any good paintings in his collection were there by accident. Did you ever hear the story about his Modigliani?"

"Vaguely," Argyll confessed. "It was destroyed, wasn't it?"

"Typical of the man. Too weak to do anything about his wife having an affair with him, but becomes outraged when he paints her in the nude. People might *suspect,* you see. Couldn't have that; nothing else mattered to him. It was all appearances with him."

"This picture . . . ?"

"Finzi knew what it was by instinct; I could prove it after I'd worked on the matter a little. I had it all down, tracked down the preparatory sketches in the Uffizi, identified the print by Passarotti; but I never published. Couldn't; wouldn't as long as it was in the hands of that man. Stonehouse didn't have a clue; he relied on that old fraud Berenson, who gave him an invented attribution as a joke. Berenson knew perfectly well what it was, but would rather have died than tell him. Stonehouse never had a sense of humor and could certainly never tell when he was being made fun of. I took it on impulse when I saw where he'd hung it. That was the final insult. Had it been mine, I would have cleared out every other picture in the entire place, and just had that, hanging in the best position I could find. Not tucked away in some little bedroom surrounded by rubbish."

Argyll now had a ticklish problem on his hands. He had the picture, or rather Bottando did; Bulovius had the identity. Joining the two together might be more difficult than it seemed. People often make the mistake of thinking that art dealing is all about art. It isn't; it is all about information, and the person who knows what a picture is generally is in a stronger position than the one who merely owns it. Bulovius knew this as well as Argyll did; better, in fact. It was so deeply ingrained in him that he would not disclose what he knew as a matter of honor unless he got something in return. It was Argyll's task now to prize the more important part of the equation out of his grasp.

"Let me get this straight, please," he said, ignoring the problem for the time being. "You arrive at the villa, already knowing this picture was there and planning to take it . . ."

"No, no," he said testily. "What do you think I am? I knew it was there, naturally. Finzi had mentioned it on many occasions and I was looking forward to seeing it. I was in quite a tremor when I didn't notice it in any of the main rooms. Finzi never considered that Stonehouse had kept it merely to prevent him from having it. If he'd loved it and couldn't bear to part with it, then he might have been forgiven."

He stopped. Damnation, Jonathan thought. Another few words and he might have come out with the name.

"Anyway, when I finally spotted it, sandwiched between a hideous portrait and a print, I was horrified. And contemptuous. It was very naughty of me, but I decided to teach him a lesson. If he didn't know what it was, he wouldn't miss it."

"So you took it."

Bulovius heaved a sigh. "I did. And I must say I can quite see the appeal of a life of crime. It was terribly exciting, sneaking around in the middle of the night on tiptoe, hiding the picture. Although a bit nerve-racking. I was quite a-flutter by the end."

"Where did you put it?"

"Oh, nowhere very sophisticated. I'm afraid I'm not so imaginative about that sort of thing. I might have done better had I thought a bit more, but I spent so much time screwing up my courage to take it, I didn't really think about what to do next. Stonehouse had a huge settee in the salon; ugly, but the only comfortable thing in the entire room. I put it under there. No one had cleaned under it for years; I almost woke the entire house with sneezing when I stuffed it under. It gave me a bit of a shock the next day when I saw that policeman sitting on it."

"So how did it get into the ditch?"

"I don't know. All I know is that, after I removed it from Stonehouse, someone removed it from me. And then I watched from my window as one of the policemen and that Verney woman strolled across the garden, straight to the ditch where it was found. And found it."

Argyll's recovery from the shock was impressive. Scarcely a blink. Not even a slight stammer, let alone anything more melo-dramatic, like an audible groan, or beating his breast and falling to the floor, even though, in his opinion, all would have been perfectly excusable. He should have known, of course, that Mary Verney would have been involved; how, exactly, still seemed hopelessly obscure to him.

"What Verney woman was this?" he asked with a lack of inter-est that made him feel rather proud.

"She was some sort of student. Pretty girl, though a bit pert for my taste. A bit too clever, if you understand me. And far too much in the company of the police for my liking. I only remember her because she knew a dealer friend of mine."

"What do you mean, 'in the company of the police'?"

Bulovius chortled and gave Argyll a knowing wink, which was a remarkably repulsive sight on the ancient face.

"Too fond of them, if you see what I mean. She looked like a young innocent, but always seemed to know far more than she let on."

Vague and unhelpful, but then Bulovius didn't really want to be helpful. "I see," Argyll said. "But this picture . . ."

"That's all I can tell you," he replied. "The policeman handed it over in triumph, much to the obvious irritation of his rather bump-tious superior officer, and as far as I know the matter was dropped. The police came up with some theory that the thieves had pan-icked and dropped it as they fled. Complete nonsense, of course, and I'm sure that young man knew it as well. He was protecting me, it seemed, which was very agreeable of him, although I can't think why he did. Whatever, the police, Stonehouse, and I were all happy for the matter to be dropped, and dropped it was. End of story."

He paused and sipped his whiskey with such obvious relish that Argyll was glad he'd let him have it. Once the complete thrill of pleasure had coursed around the old man's frail body, Argyll tried again to broach the real subject.

"Your identification. You're sure about it?"

"Of course. I know you think it is just my fancy; it isn't. Compare the one in Fiesole, look at the style, and above all, read your Vasari. There is no doubt about it at all; enough evidence to convince even the most skeptical. Overwhelming, once you put it all together. Many paintings are attributed on far less evidence. If Finzi could only have completed it . . ."

Argyll was trembling with frustration. All he had to do was take the plunge. What in God's name is it? He had to ask quietly, although he felt like screaming. But he knew what would happen. Bulovius would clam up. In fact, the faintest twinkle in the old rogue's eye suggested he knew perfectly well what was going on. He might eventually cough up, but not until Argyll worked for it.

He pushed and probed for a while longer, but then gave up for fear of making the old man dig in his heels. Then he left as graciously as possible, and stumped cursing down the stairs. He went to Bottando's apartment, and leaned on the bell for longer than was necessary in the hope that Bottando had returned and could let him in so he could study the picture again. But no luck. The general was still away, and an inch of wood reinforced with steel plate prevented him from getting in.

He went to bed no wiser; and when he decided to take the chance the next day and ask Bulovius a straight question, he was met at the door by the old man's nurse. Tancred Bulovius, she said in a sorrowful voice, had died in the night, probably because the old soak had somehow managed to get hold of some whiskey.

12

For Flavia, the first indication of trouble came around about the same time that Argyll was listening with mounting discomfort to the nurse's tale of Bulovius's last moments. It was two o'clock in the afternoon, and the loathsome journalist had rung back.

"I was wondering," he began, "if I might have your comments on a story we're thinking of printing."

"Go ahead," Flavia said. "If I can, I will."

"It is about the theft and ransom of a painting from the National Museum."

Flavia's heart took a little leap downward; her stomach flipped over.

"Do tell," she said. "It's the first I've heard of it."

"Really?" Dossoni sounded unconvinced. "We have it on good authority that a painting to be shown in the forthcoming exhibition of European art was hijacked by a band of armed robbers, who escaped despite the heroic efforts of guards to stop them . . ."

"What did the guards do?"

"Apparently, our sources say they hurled themselves on one robber, and only stopped resisting when the thieves threatened to shoot one of them."

"Very courageous of them," Flavia said.

"The painting disappeared, then reappeared a week later. A ransom had obviously been paid."

"Obviously. If any of this is true. What does the museum say?"

"I haven't talked to them yet."

"Your source for this is one of the heroic guards, I assume?"

"I couldn't possibly tell you that. Can you confirm the story?"

"No. In fact, I can deny all knowledge of it."

"There was no theft?"

"Don't be ridiculous. How long could you keep that quiet?"

"No ransom paid?"

"Not by me. You asked me this a week ago, if you remember. I told you then that it was illegal, and that we don't have access to money like that. How much were these guards paid?"

"We never pay for stories," he said. "We don't have much money either. But I was told the guards were hauled up in front of you and told to keep their mouths shut."

"Didn't do a very good job, then, did I?"

"No. Nor did you answer my question. Did an armed gang steal a painting from the museum last week?"

"Absolutely not."

"Did you pay a ransom to get it back?"

"Absolutely not. There was no armed gang stealing anything from the museum last week. Or the week before."

"Any other comments?"

"Yes. Never trust the word of guards. Heroic or otherwise."

She put the phone down and frowned, murderous thoughts on her mind. It was only a matter of time before Dossoni amended his questions and got the story right. She wasn't responsible for it, but she sensed stormy waters ahead. In the circumstances, she thought it a good idea to forewarn the prime minister. And to shout at Macchioli for his inability to control his staff.

Then she went home and found a disconsolate Argyll, who

promptly confessed to her that he was, to all intents and purposes, a murderer.

"I gave him the whiskey. For heaven's sake! How could I have been so stupid?"

She was not sympathetic.

"I feel terrible about it," he went on.

"Because you killed him or because he didn't tell you what that picture is," she asked dryly.

"Mainly the first. But the second doesn't help. What do you think about Bottando? His knowing Mary Verney. He never mentioned it the last time when you wanted to arrest her, did he?"

"No. But it may be that he didn't make the connection. After all, it doesn't seem as though she was suspected of anything back in 1962. She was never questioned, or anything. Just a witness. And I can't remember the names of witnesses I talked to forty days ago, let alone forty years."

"Hmph." Argyll was unconvinced. Anything and everything to do with Mary Verney made him quiver a little. Her mere existence, in his opinion, was a nightmare. He had not yet forgiven her for the fact that she was so very good at seeming a sweet, harmless, and slightly eccentric lady of a certain age, most concerned with blackfly on roses and the current state of the village church restoration appeal. As a result, he tended to overestimate her capacity to cause him grief. If the angel of the lord came down to blow a mighty trump and announce the end of the world, Argyll would easily have believed Mary Verney was, somehow, responsible for the event for obscure reasons of her own. And his opinion of her was high enough to think that even at a distance of nearly forty years, her deeds could cause mayhem.

"The trouble is that she was there. Now Bulovius's dead, she's my only hope. Bottando at least seems genuinely to have no notion that the picture was anything in particular."

"Which it might not be."

"True." He thought, then shook off the feeling of glum foreboding that had descended on him ever since he heard of Mary's presence at the Villa Buonaterra in 1962. "Go on, then. What's on your mind?"

"Nothing of importance in comparison to you," she replied, with a mild hint of acid in her voice. "Just journalists and paintings and ransoms. I'm beginning to feel vulnerable."

Argyll nodded when she had summarized her day. "You might have mentioned it before I went rabbitting on, you know," he said reproachfully. "What are you going to do about it?"

She shrugged. "Nothing. What can I do? Either the paper publishes its story, or it doesn't. I've done my best, and can at least point to the fact that I did say it was inevitable. Smash and grab raids on museums are hard to keep quiet forever. However, that doesn't mean I won't take the blame."

"What for?"

"They'll think of something. Allowing the robbery to happen. Paying a ransom against the express orders of the prime minister. Failing to keep those stupid guards quiet. Not arresting the robber while he was still alive. Something like that. Or maybe nothing. Maybe they'll just ease me out; there are plenty of people who want my job, after all. This gives them a perfect opportunity."

She stood up and stretched. "And there really is nothing I can do. Except try and find the money. In which case I might be able to count on Di Lanna to put in a good word. Or, then again, maybe not. He seems to want the whole thing dropped as well."

"Sounds like good advice to me."

"You won't say that when this Dossoni character runs his story."

"You don't seem too concerned."

"I'm not, oddly enough. I don't know why. Maybe it's Bottando's going. He was always the great inspiration. Dedication, you know. I worked for him more than the department. Even when he went, I always thought he was still in charge really."

"So he was, in theory."

"But he packed his bags and walked away, without a moment's regret, it seems. And if he can do it after so many years, why am I so enthusiastic? What does it matter, anyway, running round chasing after pictures?"

"Not a positive attitude."

"No. But there must be something more worthwhile to do."

"What?"

She thought. "I don't know."

She nibbled at a piece of cheese, then sat down again. "Meanwhile, I'll fill in the hours by going to Siena tomorrow. Records has produced the address of an old comrade-in-arms of Sabbatini. It's probably a waste of time, but you never know."

13

The drive to Siena was uneventful, even pleasant. It is very hard to be preoccupied and worried when you have the distractions of Italian traffic constantly threatening to force you off the road if your attention wanders too much. The address she had was for a small village about twenty kilometers to the northeast, but she stopped in the town anyway to have some lunch and also to look at the language school where Elena Fortini, Sabbatini's former colleague, now worked. Her file said she was half American and half Italian and spoke English fluently. This skill now gained her a living, and a very quiet living it must be, Flavia thought to herself. Anybody who buried herself here must be looking for a quiet life.

This woman had been an artist of a sort back in the 1970s as well, although then she had produced the sort of art which rarely engaged Flavia's official attention. She had been an ideological soul mate for Sabbatini and reading between the lines of the file Corrado had found for her, Flavia guessed that she had been the brains behind his politics. While she sensed that Sabbatini had been a radical because it was fashionable, this woman had been more serious, her opinions and actions more carefully thought through, even reasonable. Sabbatini had followed her lead and acted as he did to draw attention to himself.

As with many of the people who had been in revolutionary

movements in the 1970s, Elena had realized, perhaps earlier than most, that the battle would never be won. Consequently, she had taken up an offer of a pardon in return for a brief prison sentence, a full confession, and information about her erstwhile colleagues. A notice attached to the file expressed irritation that the amount of information she gave was minimal, and completely unhelpful. Even when saving her own skin, she was unprepared to give up her friends.

Finding her had been remarkably easy; once a political criminal, always a political criminal, and Fortini was required to register her address every six months even though it hadn't changed for years. The latest address was attached to another file Flavia had extracted from colleagues in antiterrorism.

Once she had eaten, rested, and prepared herself she drove the rest of the trip to where the woman lived. The house was a small and run-down pile, one of those difficult structures that is clearly old but could have been built anywhere between the fifteenth and the eighteenth centuries. Not big, but with bits added on here and there, so that the roofscape of terra-cotta tiles headed up and down in all directions and at all angles. Valuable now that so many English and Germans and Dutch wanted summer houses; bought for a song ten or twenty years ago and now worth a fortune.

All the stereotypes that built up in her mind so easily began to break down as Flavia walked to the door and saw the piles of chicken feed stacked neatly on the little terrace, the washing line covered in children's clothes, and as she took in the general air of impoverishment—a tile missing here, a large crack in the thick stone wall there—that hung about the place. Not neglect, though; everything had a well-loved air to it.

The signs of activity were all around; from the other side of the house came the unmistakable sounds of children playing, scream-ing with laughter amid the splashing of water; two hens strutted neurotically around, their beady eyes fixed on the ground, intent on spotting every last fleck of food; a cat slept peacefully nearby, ignoring everything. From inside came the sound of a woman singing to herself—obviously to herself, as no one would ever dare sing that badly in anybody else's hearing. The house had all the signs of poor owners, of making do, of there being little luxury. Flavia felt an enormous and uncontrollable surge of longing. Some people make comfort and contentment wherever they are, whatever their circumstances. This house was created by one of those people. Her surprise was as great as her envy.

The singing stopped abruptly when she knocked; there was a long pause, then a woman in her late forties came to the open door, drying her hands as she walked.

She even had a pleasant face, this terrorist ideologue. She had once been striking. Now the face was getting old, careworn with tiredness. But again, there was an ease and a contentment there that came from a deeper place.

"Elena Fortini?" Flavia asked. "May I have a word with you, please?"

There was instant suspicion, but no fear or uncertainty in the response. "Secret police come to check on my bomb-making factory, are you? Come in, then."

Flavia stepped over the threshold, into the warm hospitality and the domesticity of others. "Police, but not very secret," she said. "I'd like to see the bomb-making factory, though. I love these country pursuits."

Elena eyed her carefully, paused a second, then let out a laugh. "Later, if you want."

She led the way to the huge stone-floored room that served as kitchen, workroom, laundry room, dining room, and sitting room. In one corner a television, in another a piano jammed up against a washing machine so old it should have been in a museum. Surrounding it was so much washing that Flavia felt a pang of sympathy for the machine.

"Dirty things, children," Elena said. "I live my life cocooned in washing."

"How many do you have?"

"Two. I know; you thought there must be at least eight to produce this mess. But two is quite enough to reduce anything to rubble. I have a vague image of tidiness I keep in my mind, rather like some people have a notion of eternity in paradise. You never approach it, but it's good to believe that you might get there one day."

She gestured for Flavia to sit down at the table while she poured some coffee. "The English maintain that old age begins when the police start looking young," she commented.

"Sounds like a compliment to me," Flavia said. "I feel anything but young at the moment."

Elena peered at her carefully, then nodded. "I'm not surprised," she said elliptically. "I suppose if I told you to go away, it wouldn't do any good."

"Sorry, no. But I don't think I'll take up much time. We don't bother you much, do we?"

"More than you should. It's not as if I ever have anything new to say to you, after all."

"Maybe this time you will. I'm here to ask you about more recent events. In the last month."

"I've scarcely been out of the house in the last month."

"Visitors?"

"I don't encourage them."

"Phone calls?"

"No phone."

"Letters?"

"Only bills. Listen, why don't you ask proper questions? Then I might be able to answer more usefully."

"Very well. Maurizio Sabbatini."

Elena rolled her eyes. "I might have known. What's the old faker been up to now?"

"He's dead, for one thing."

She grimaced. "So I heard." She rubbed her nose for a few seconds and concentrated hard, so it seemed, to keep the tears out of her eyes. "He was a complete fraud, you know. A faker in everything he thought and said and did. He had the sincerity of a beetle, and the constancy of an earthworm. I hadn't seen him for ten years, never wanted to see him again, and I'm very upset he's dead. Can you explain that?"

"Part of your past goes with him?"

"Glib and facile."

"Yes, but I don't know anything about either of you. Glib and facile is all I can manage."

"He was fun. Always laughing. Even when he robbed a bank, he thought it an absolute hoot. And made everyone else laugh as well. He even had the bank manager in stitches before he left. He used to come to collective meetings, when everyone was earnestly discussing the dictatorship of the proletariat, and within half an hour had everybody giggling hysterically. He could never take anything seriously."

"So why didn't you want to see him again?"

"Life is not a laugh. Some things are too serious."

There was a lot, a whole world, unsaid here. Flavia waited, hoping she would volunteer the information, but instead she just looked up at her. "And he's dead, and you're here. Perhaps you'd better tell me why?"

"I was hoping you'd tell me."

"Maybe I can. Maybe I will. But you can hardly expect me to pour out my soul to some policewoman who just walks in my door one day. I don't know who you are or what you want. Anything I say you'll have to earn. Don't you think that's fair?"

It wasn't. She was a convicted criminal, Flavia was police. She should answer all questions put to her. In theory. Flavia realized quite well that this was not the right approach. Elena Fortini, she knew, had withstood more seasoned, more brutal interrogators than she would ever be. Anything she wanted that this woman knew would have to be given up freely or not at all.

"Earn how?"

"By telling me why you're interested in such a wastrel. Tell me about my poor old clown. Then maybe I will tell you about him myself. It's not as if you can do him any harm, and not as if I'd care much even if you could."

So Flavia told her a little: about the theft of the painting, how someone else had swapped the picture for the ransom, how Sabbatini was already dead by then. No details, just an outline.

"Was there an autopsy? Was he drunk?"

"Fairly drunk. Not gigantically so, though. Not to induce a stupor, I would have thought. But enough to make him fall asleep and stay asleep as he drowned."

"You've considered the possibility that he was held under until he drowned?"

Flavia hadn't. Indeed, the idea had never crossed her mind, so easy had it been to summon up an image of a dissipated, irresponsible fake artist incapable even of staying awake in a bath. So she reconsidered quickly.

"If it was the case, then it is likely to go down as the perfect murder. No one saw, heard, or suspected anything. There is not the slightest shred of evidence."

She nodded. "Just like last time, then."

Flavia raised an eyebrow.

"His sister," she explained.

"Ah. That I know about."

Elena looked closely at her. "I wonder why," she said.

"Tell me about it, though. I don't know many of the details," Flavia prompted.

"Find them yourself. It's all in the file, isn't it? Young innocent murdered by ruthless terrorists?"

"Is that why you stopped? If I remember, she was killed in 1981, you gave yourself up soon afterward."

She shrugged. "My womanly instincts revolted, is that what you think? No; I gave up because I hate lost causes. No other reason. Besides, I thought you were here to discuss the present, not the past."

"I'm here to discuss Sabbatini."

"Maurizio was a joker, unreliable, untrustworthy. He doted on his sister, and when he was picked up by the police, she was kidnapped to warn him to keep his mouth closed. Then she was killed. He never quite recovered from it; he felt responsible, which he was. He stopped laughing. Is that good enough for you?"

Flavia got up and poured herself another coffee without asking. It was very strange how she felt at home here, companionable with this incomprehensible woman, so sweet and gentle, and with such a past. Flavia over the years had come to trust her feelings for people; if she felt comfortable with them, it usually meant they were trustworthy, even pleasant. This time her feelings and what she had just heard were so mismatched that nothing was making sense.

"So how did you get here?"

"I retired," she said with a faint smile. "I couldn't take it anymore. There were only two ways to go: ever more violence in a cause that was becoming hopeless, or getting out. I got out; others chose a different course."

"And Maurizio?"

"You know as much as I do. It has struck you, I suppose, that the theft of this painting mirrors his past antics? That he advertised himself so that it must have been clear—to some people if not to you—who was responsible?"

Flavia nodded. "And the money?"

"Maurizio was never interested in money."

Flavia shook her head. "I'm out of my depth here. I can't even begin to see the logic of this. I'm used to people doing things for simple reasons, even good reasons. Wanting more money is the main one."

Elena shrugged. She got up, peered through the window into the sunlight where the children were playing, and began to tidy the kitchen. She had said her piece.

"You asked, I answered. Nothing more I can say. But the idea that Maurizio was after money doesn't work. Nor does the idea that he was working with someone. He never did in the past, not even with me. He trusted absolutely no one. No friends, no colleagues. And you are telling me that he suddenly got himself an accomplice and suddenly became interested in money. Very unlikely. But," she said as she walked Flavia back to the car, "you must make up your own mind. Tell me one thing, though," she said as she watched Flavia open the door and prepare to leave.

"Yes?"

"Boy or girl?"

Flavia frowned in puzzlement. "What?"

"The baby. Is it a boy or a girl?"

14

As far as Argyll was concerned, Flavia had merely gone off on a routine expedition and would be back, that day or the next, when she had finished. There was no need to hang about waiting for her when there were things to be done. And many of the things that were to be done were proving rather difficult. He rang his old employer in London to see if there were any papers about the Finzi collection around, but was told what he already suspected, that they had all been left to Tancred Bulovius. He decided not to explain why he didn't feel it right to try and look at them just now. So he asked for a list of the Finzi paintings bequeathed to the London National Gallery instead, just to get a feel for the man's tastes.

And he gave a summary of his conversation with Bulovius, to see if Byrnes had any suggestions.

"This picture I told you about. Bulovius said it was hugely important, but I couldn't get the old buffer to come clean. Unless I can get some sort of hint . . ."

"No one else has ever seen anything in it?"

"Not many people have ever looked at it. Not in the last half century, anyway. Bulovius said it was obvious when you looked at it, but it wasn't to me. What do you think?"

"Possible," Byrnes said. "He was immensely knowledgeable. Unfortunately, he never published much, or wrote much down."

IAIN PEARS

Argyll groaned.

"And," Byrnes went on to make things worse, "there aren't many people who knew as much as he did. He had an uncommonly good eye. His say-so would mean a lot."

Argyll ground his teeth.

"You're being very noisy," Byrnes said disapprovingly.

"It reflects my sense of frustration. I suspect I am dealing with one of the most important pictures I have ever come across, but I don't know what it is, and can't find out."

"I'll have a look if you like. See if anything springs to mind."

"Thank you. But unless I get a handle on Bulovius's proof, it's still all opinion. Damnation."

"What?"

"Nothing." Argyll thanked him and put the phone down, cursed for a bit and then did some more phoning. And then he, too, packed an overnight bag and, as Flavia had taken the car, headed for the railway station.

It was premature of him; he arrived far too late to do anything of use, and had to spend the evening wandering about Florence killing time and grumbling about the unnecessary expense of a hotel room for the night when he could have been at home in bed. But the idea of Florence had appealed, and by the time he realized it wasn't such a good one it was too late.

Once upon a time, and not very long ago, he would have considered few things nicer than spending an evening in Florence, all alone, not doing very much. He'd spent much of his life, certainly many of the enjoyable parts of it, doing something similar in several dozen cities across Europe. But he had noticed that the charms of solitude were beginning to pall a bit. He got lonely more easily and more quickly. He missed someone to talk to. He found his own company at a table in a restaurant a bit tedious. He went to bed early, and read the copy of Vasari's *Lives* he had brought with him.

He was still feeling slightly disconcerted by the failure of old pleasures when he got up the next morning and walked over to the Church of San Pietro that Bulovius had mentioned. No help there. Then he hired a car (another unnecessary expense) and struggled through the morning traffic to Fiesole. And here it all came together. Of course it did. The Church of San Francesco was a Franciscan church. And there, in a prominent place, was a version of the Immaculate Conception—again with atypical imagery, not the same at all but fitting what he was looking for.

Out came the Vasari, and there, plain as a pikestaff once you knew where to look, was the reference to *un nostro donna con figure,* which in 1550 was in the Church of San Pietro. And it wasn't there anymore. No one had ever heard of it.

He went and found an agreeable seat overlooking Florence, and thought about it. It wasn't conclusive; all it did was demonstrate what Bulovius thought the picture was. But now that he had a name, he could follow up at the Uffizi and check the drawing Bulovius had mentioned. Then he'd be close.

His head still spinning, he got back in his car and drove northward. His destination was Poggio di Amoretta, a hamlet more than a village, perched on top of a hill fifteen kilometers outside Florence, and about three from the Villa Buonaterra. It took rather longer than it should have to get there, partly because of the traffic, but more because Argyll got lost, and then stopped minding; it is hard to keep your mind on business when you find yourself in the wrong village, squashed in a tiny square facing the unfinished facade of a Romanesque church with a door beckoningly open— come in and see—together with a minuscule restaurant with an aged waiter hopefully setting out clean, pressed table linen for diners who seemed unlikely to show up.

Argyll's mood was restored in an instant. It was eleven forty-five, and May. It was warm, but the air still had none of the harshness of afternoon. Apart from the waiter, there was no sound at all; Argyll could even hear the reassuring rumble of a tractor from way over the next hill. The vines were neat, ordered, trimmed, and ready to do their best. There was no choice really. What was the point of being in Italy unless you took advantage of such things? And, for only the second time in more than a decade, as he breathed in the clean, fresh air, he thought that life in Rome was, perhaps, not so perfect after all. That there were disadvantages; that the noise, the smell, and the crowds were not so completely trumped by the pleasures of the place.

He got out of the car, nodded amiably at the waiter, discovered that there would be no food for another half hour at least, then puttered into the church, coming out twenty minutes later with his air of relaxed contentment perfectly reestablished. A lovely little thing, delightful altarpiece, and some handsome sculpture. As usual, he thought wistfully that, had he really been lucky, he would have been born a Tuscan master mason, around about 1280. The best possible job in the most civilized of all periods. Must be nice to build a church.

A glass of cool fine wine, some homemade pasta, a little piece of veal, and two coffees erased any remaining sense of urgency. He chatted with the waiter—who had little else to do—then to the waiter's wife, who had made the pasta and cooked the meal. Then he just sat and watched and listened. A goat walked past. It was very interesting.

He didn't really fall asleep, just dozed a little, but it was formidably difficult to get up, and he did so only when the clock on the church tower struck a halfhearted two o'clock. He looked at his watch. It was quarter past. Disaster. He went inside, found the phone and called Flavia to say he'd be late. No answer, so he left a message. Then he stretched, ambled back to his car and drove the remaining kilometer to Poggio di Amoretta.

The reasoning that brought him there was more or less sound, in theory: he had finally got hold of someone in Weller, the Norfolk village where Mary Verney lived, who had some idea where she was. Not in England; in fact, he was told that she was at her house in Tuscany. Where this house was, unfortunately, was unknown. But here he was, nevertheless, simply on the basis of Stonehouse's memory that at the time of the Buonaterra robbery she had been mainly staying in the village of Poggio di Amoretta, and on her own recent statement that she wanted to come and stay in a house she owned.

And this is where Argyll came, long shot though it was. But, as he kept on telling himself, the reasoning was not entirely stupid; it was based more on what he considered to be a profound knowledge of Mary Verney's character and common sense. Besides which, she had to have lived somewhere before she inherited the great pile in Norfolk—prematurely, and only by murdering its previous occupant, admittedly—and her Italian was so perfect that long years of residence in the country could be assumed.

A fine, indeed an elegant, piece of reasoning of which he was inordinately proud. On top of it, of course (although he played this down in his mind so as to heighten the satisfaction produced by the contemplation of his deductive powers), was the fact that a Signora Maria Verney was listed in the phone book.

So he arrived in the village, parked, asked directions, and, as the path was steep and not really suitable for cars, walked the rest of the way. From three hundred meters he could see Mary Verney, sitting on the little terrace in a sun hat. From two hundred meters he could see that she had a visitor. Damnation.

He slowed down, stopped, and then thought carefully about what he should do; for reasons he didn't fully understand, he suddenly felt reluctant to intrude, although what exactly he would be intruding into escaped him. For a while he stood there, shifting uneasily from leg to leg, then he turned on his heel and walked back the way he had come.

Argyll had had the experience once before, and had always

hoped to taste it again. It was with a painting he'd bought, a landscape with a few figures dancing in the foreground. Old, dirty, inexpensive; he'd had it cleaned and restored as inexpensively as he could manage and when it came back from the workshop he stacked it in a corner of the apartment, in a place where Flavia would not put her foot through it in a moment of absentmindedness, and all but forgot about it. Then, one morning, he spent some time staring it at, and got a prickle of excitement running down his back. He recognized the pose of one of the figures dancing merrily in the shaft of sunlight the painter had put across the canvas.

As far as he was concerned, no more was necessary: he was as sure of the authorship as if he'd seen the man paint it himself. It was, most certainly, a Salvator Rosa; not great, not brilliant, no masterpiece to set the world alight, and, indeed, even when he'd finally pinned it down, the picture scarcely made him any money once all the costs had been taken into account. In the eyes of the auctioneers and the collectors who insist on bits of paper, there was always that element of doubt, enough to refuse the little work a solid name and title. No matter; it was the pleasure of certainty which Argyll had enjoyed, the fact that instinct told him where to look, and eventually led him to a sketch for the dancing woman, hand held high, head slightly angled to one side, her blue dress billowing as she danced to the music of the lyre.

He had hoped to experience the same sensation with the little picture now on Bottando's wall, but nothing except a prickle of interest had come when he'd first seen it, and he hadn't been able to have another look. To experience that tingle of excitement unexpectedly now, seeing a sixty-year-old woman two hundred meters away on her terrace, turning her head to greet her visitor, was so unexpected he found it shocking. Perhaps it was again the turn of the head, the way her arm momentarily echoed the roll of the hillside beyond— the sort of trick Rosa himself might have pulled off. Maybe again it was the dappled effect of the light, which gave a timeless, almost impressionistic glimpse of other people's contentment that almost took his breath away.

About a mile farther on, halfway up a hill, he saw a little chapel, standing at the edge of what seemed like a reasonable track, one of those places built long ago for reasons which no one can now remember. He started walking up to it. The air and the exercise might, he thought vaguely, make him think more clearly. It would at least gain him some time. So, hands in pockets, head down, off he walked, taking his time.

As he walked, his imagination went into overdrive; he scarcely noticed the path and when he came back down again he had no idea whether he'd been walking for twenty minutes or two hours. Much of what he imagined had no facts to support it. It didn't matter, nor was it important if the details had happened differently. His imagination painted the scene, filled in the details, elaborated on what he knew, suspected, and guessed. What Stonehouse had said, Bulovius, the police report. What he knew of Mary Verney and of Bottando, what was reasonable and what was possible. He could now see those long-ago events in a black and white that was slightly grainy; Argyll's imagination had been formed by too many Italian neo-realist films to imagine Tuscany, 1962, in any other way.

The painting had vanished from the Villa Buonaterra and, after some little delay during which all present had looked for it, the police had been summoned. The meeting was an inauspicious one, even as he replayed it in his mind. The little police car, some sort of Fiat, he decided, old, gray, and battered, with smoke pouring out of its rear end, chugs noisily and with little dignity up to the grand entranceway, lurching to a halt and shuddering into quiet with an alarming death rattle that shakes the bones of the two occupants. One of these, the older, dressed in civilian clothes that show considerable wear, leads the way to the door. The other, much younger and in a tight-fitting uniform, which makes him look even less comfortable than he feels, follows obediently. They do not talk; position has to be maintained. Instead, the senior figure stands aside and nods at the bell. His subordinate steps forward to ring it, an impassive face showing neither resentment nor the contempt he feels so keenly. It is already desperately hot; the police report didn't mention it, but it is July and Tuscany. Of course it is hot.

The servant opens the door and, though the two are expected, he goes through the formality of asking them their business, showing them into a small room that exists solely for accommodating new arrivals whose precise status is uncertain, and goes off to announce their presence to the owner, who has in fact, seen the car arrive perfectly clearly from the window of his study.

Commissario Tarento fidgets, or at least Argyll imagines he fidgets, in the way a small-town policeman would under such circumstances. He is more used to bicycle thieves than art thieves. Both crime and victim are far beyond him. So he tries to seem brusque and impatient. The natural, uncontrollable deference that flows through his veins like lifeblood, which took him into the police in the first place, wells up in him; a combination of pride, envy, and respect for those richer and more comfortable than himself is part of his nature, even part of his generation. Foreign grandees of unimaginable wealth bring it out in full force; he can only imagine—and does so, frequently—the life of elegance and leisure they lead.

Oddly, his subordinate seems more at ease now there is more than the commissario to take his attention. Why this is so Tarento cannot imagine. For he knows Bottando's background well: a poor family from a village north of Naples—respectable but with an uncle who is a communist. Bottando had gone into the army, then into the police, to escape a life that had held nothing for his parents and would hold nothing for him. It was a choice: the military or the factories of Turin and Milan, which were crying out for southern labor. Even as an adolescent, Bottando had thought there was more to life, possibly, than a fat wage packet and an apartment where the concrete was still damp from the hasty construction.

Tarento does not like the young man, although he cannot say why; his behavior is impeccable, his efforts unsparing, and his aptitude considerable. That, perhaps, is the problem, for Tarento has reached the peak of his career, and knows it. Even in a force riddled with corruption and incompetence, he has reached his level. Not so Bottando, who has already attracted the attention of the prosecuting magistrate; if he can bear it, the young man will rise—farther and faster than Tarento. The realization of this, and the fact that already Bottando has more self-confidence and assurance than his superior has, made the older man harsh and rude, going out of his way to impose his seniority while he still possesses it.

At least he manages to suppress a little bow and an obsequious smile when Stonehouse comes in to welcome them with all the grace and elegance of nobility, for Tarento is unaware of the great subtleties of English class distinctions. Instead, he takes his seat with a flourish, as though sitting in a *seicento* chair covered in fine Brussels tapestry is quite normal for him. He even makes a comment on its beauty, but notices that, somehow, his effort comes across less well than Bottando's indifferent silence as he also sits down. Stonehouse acknowledges the compliment but a brief, unsettling look of vague puzzlement passes across his face at the words. It is enough to make Tarento lose the little assurance he possesses.

So, he tries to become professional, the representative of the Italian state, with all the might of the law behind him, almost barking questions that are answered, in flawless Italian, with courtesy and concision.

There has been, Stonehouse says, a theft of a small painting. It was noticed that morning and he contacted the police directly.

"And the item removed?"

Stonehouse picks up a sheaf of paper from the desk: Argyll imagined it being part of the carefully handwritten inventory still in the Buonaterra muniments room. "I got this out for you," he says. "I have a description of all my collection. It is a painting on wood of a Madonna. Florentine, fifteenth century, but of no great importance. Not compared to some of the other pictures in the house."

"And the artist?"

"Unknown, although my friend Mr. Berenson gave it one of his own attributions. I do not think his efforts are very helpful, however. More important is that it is quite small—easily carried by one person—and was taken out of its frame in a responsible manner. The thief took his time, and was concerned not to damage it."

"It is my job to ascertain what is important," Tarento says stiffly, and is pleased to see Stonehouse acknowledge his error. "What elements of security do you possess?"

"None."

Tarento affects to look surprised, although there is no cause; this was not yet the time when anyone, rich or poor, felt much need to defend themselves from the outside world.

"In fact," Stonehouse continues, "all the windows were wide open. The maid judged that there would be no rain last night— rightly, as it turned out—and opened everything up to try and blow some of this hideous heat out of the place."

He is right there, Tarento thinks; the heat in the past fortnight has been oppressive to a degree he can hardly remember, a dull, weakening heat that dampens the spirits and slows brain and body together.

"The maid opens the window, and allows the burglars in," Tarento says knowingly. "I shall have to talk to this woman." Maids are something Tarento knows about, his wife having been in service with a grand Florentine family until she married him.

"No doubt," Stonehouse says. "But you should know in advance that she is sixty-five, has been with my family here for twenty years, and is of impeccable character. I do not and will not entertain any suspicions of her."

"Nonetheless, she must be interviewed," Tarento replies firmly.

"Whatever you wish," Stonehouse says. "Would you like a glass of wine? Water?"

The prospect of a drink, of becoming acquainted on more friendly terms, is irresistible; Tarento imagines himself sipping away, gradually winning the respect, even the regard of this man, becoming almost familiar. But not with Bottando there to watch; he chooses a glass of wine.

"And while we talk, perhaps my subordinate could tour the grounds. Footprints, you know. That is the sort of thing he is very good at."

He speaks confidingly, as if Bottando isn't there, as if he is a pet spaniel. And Bottando obediently gets up and salutes and does as he is told, leaving the two men alone.

In Argyll's imagination, Bottando goes through the motions, for although the orders deserve nothing but contempt—the earth is baked hard as concrete and you could have driven a tank over it without leaving any mark—he is not yet sure enough to treat them as such. And so he stares briefly at the gravel, the browned piece of grass, the wilting hedges, then gazes at the house to try and figure out which room had contained the stolen painting.

"That one," says a cheerful voice behind him. He turns to see who has spoken.

"Top floor, second from the left," the voice continues, and the young woman who owns it, holding a straw hat on her head with one hand, points with the other. Then she smiles engagingly at him. An entrancing smile, impish and seductive all at once.

"Thank you," Bottando says gravely.

"Why on earth are you standing out here? You'll boil away to nothing."

"Inspecting the scene of the crime," he says, conveying in his tone of voice that he, too, knows it is a waste of time.

"I see. You stare at the house from a hundred meters, see that a chimney pot is slightly askew, and conclude that the thief parachuted onto the roof. From a glider, it must have been, as everyone was awake all night because of the heat. Someone would have heard a plane."

"Remarkable," Bottando says. "You must have read my mind."

She laughs. "It was easy. Nobody could expect to see anything else standing here."

"That's true."

"Have you seen the very scene itself? The patch on the wall where the great masterpiece used to hang? Come on, then," she says when he shakes his head. "I'll show you. Then you can sit quietly and have a cold drink. It'll be as useful as wandering around getting heatstroke."

"Are you staying in the house?" Bottando asks as they walk across the gravel path. "A member of the family?"

"Oh no," she says. "I'm a student. Friend of a friend. I'm just visiting. I have a little house twenty kilometers from here. And, as you are obviously a suspicious sort of man, that's where I was when the picture disappeared."

"You speak Italian very well."

"Thank you."

They climb the staircase slowly, lest the effort make them feel even hotter. Bottando walks behind, incapable, despite his wishes, of ignoring the girl's presence, the way she moves in her light cotton dress, so easy and relaxed.

"There," she says, flinging open a heavy door. "Now, who did it?"

She leads him into a small, brightly painted bedroom that contains little more than an old wooden bed and a heavy wardrobe. On the walls, papered with inappropriate, fusty Victorian paper, are some old prints, a portrait—exactly as the inventory said, and in fact still pretty close to how it had looked when Argyll sneaked in during his visit to the villa—and a small rectangle that is slightly lighter than its surrounds. Bottando walks across the floor—it creaked badly, Argyll had noted—and examines it closely, even though he knows it will not help at all. Then he looks around. An open window, the shutters hanging motionless on the outside, bright sunlight streaming in.

"Mr Stonehouse told the maid not to shut the shutters as she normally does. Fingerprints, he thought."

"Ah, yes," Bottando says. "Quite."

Their eyes meet and hold for a tiny fragment of a portion of a second. Just enough. Each smiles at the other at the same moment before the door swings open again and a very annoyed Commissario Tarento enters. "I told you to look around outside, Bottando," he says curtly. "Not wander about like a tourist."

"*I* insisted he come here," the girl says. "To reassure me we are in no danger. I do not like the idea of murderers and robbers wandering about the place. He has been most kind." Another mocking smile, which Bottando understands and his superior is incapable of even noticing.

Tarento is mollified and gives her a silly-little-girl look. "And you are . . ."

"Verney," she says. "My name is Mary Verney."

From that point on, Argyll's imagination concluded, everything was straightforward. No need even to go through it all. The loss of the little Virgin. Its recovery. Its reappearance on Bottando's sitting room wall. His retirement. The angle of Mary Verney's arm as she poured a glass of wine in the crisp spring sunshine. The ransoming of the Claude. Flavia's frustration at being constantly left out of things. It wasn't exactly supported by evidence, far from it; Argyll's overwrought imagination had supplied most of it. And very puzzling it all was.

15

For Flavia, not being able to get hold of Argyll was merely an irritating start to what turned into another appalling day. Around the time he was leaving for Florence, she was returning to Rome, having stayed on in Siena to tidy up a few trivial matters with the police there. She went straight to the office, where she found a note summoning her to a meeting at the ministry. Urgent, it said, and the fact that the meeting had been supposed to start five minutes previously did nothing to improve her already irritable mood. She had spent a terrible night dealing with what Elena Fortini had pointed out to her. Her condition was so obvious that she felt foolish for not having thought of it herself.

Her world had changed forever. Just like that. It was going to take some time to get used to it. She couldn't even begin to imagine how she was going to reconcile the sorts of hours that her job required with the sorts of hours that she knew from observation small children seemed to demand as their right. All she did note was that she was thinking of how to fit the job in. Not the other way around. She was still too much in a state of shock even to consider whether she was pleased or not.

She was also not really at her most attentive when she arrived, finally, at the meeting, which she thought was going to be another interminable discussion of staff training or budgets or quibbles about results. It was something about bureaucracies she had noted: the more trivial the subject, the more pompous and urgent the summons. In general, anyway. She didn't even pay enough attention to note that the two civil servants in the room—both completely unknown to her—spent a remarkable amount of time shuffling papers and looking uncomfortable.

"I'm afraid that we have to deal with more important matters now," the more senior said once the small talk had been disposed of. "That is, the future of the department now that General Bottando has left. We feel—the minister feels—that a clear leadership line is required to ensure the maintenance of the high-profile and successful performance that has been such a marked feature of the art theft department in recent years."

"I quite agree," said Flavia, still unaware of the large manhole opening up in front of her. "Staff morale, I feel, is highly important for producing the productivity gains that the ministry seems to want so much." She was very proud of that remark; it showed she was learning the language of management that seemed to be so terribly fashionable in administrative circles these days. She knew that it was all nonsense, but accepted that when in Rome it was necessary to speak a little Latin.

The other civil servant grunted and looked even more awkward. "Indeed. But that is not why we have called you here today. There is no easy way to say this, so I will not try. I regret to have to tell you that it has been decided at the highest level not to appoint you as the permanent head of the art squad."

As she did not know how to react, she scarcely reacted at all. "And may I ask the reasoning behind this decision?"

"I am afraid not," he said. "As you know, all such matters are in the strictest confidence." There was just enough of a hint of regret in his voice to make Flavia think that at least he was not enjoying himself. "The good work you have done in the past year has been noted and is greatly appreciated. Please do not think that any criticism of you or your ability is intended. However, it is thought that a figure with greater seniority is required, with, perhaps, greater willingness to adhere to policy."

"What do you mean, 'adhere to policy'?"

A faint, apologetic smile was all she got in response.

"You don't, of course, mean that I'm a woman, do you?" Flavia said.

The second civil servant had the look of a man about to be taken to the European Court of Human Rights. "Oh, dear me, no," he said in a hurry. "That's the last thing we mean."

Flavia kept quiet. The two men shuffled some more in their seats and looked at each other. They'd thought of that one. It was obvious that their approach had been worked out in advance.

"We understand that it is difficult for anybody to return to a subordinate position once they have run an organization. And we quite understand that you may consider your position untenable from now on."

It was worse than Flavia had ever imagined, even in her most paranoid nightmare. She was now paying full attention. "You want me to go away?"

"You may consider it in your own best interest and also in the best interest of the department," the man said. "I must add that to avoid any discontinuity during the transfer period, we would like the matter resolved now."

"You want me to go now?" She was even more incredulous.

There was a long pause and more fiddling on the desktop. "We can offer you two choices. The first is a transfer to a senior administrative post . . ."

"In?"

"Ah, in Bari."

"Bari?" Flavia said in disgust.

"Of course, should this not be acceptable, you might consider taking advantage of a generous severance package . . ."

"This is ridiculous," Flavia interrupted. "I have never heard of anybody being treated in such an appalling fashion. To be passed over, I suppose, is something that happens. Although, to be perfectly frank, I do not know of anyone who could do the job as well as I can. But to be ejected so unceremoniously, almost as though I had been caught with my hand in the till or something like that, is outrageous."

"I knew this was not going to be easy or pleasant for any of us," the first civil servant replied regretfully. "All I can say is that you have our considerable sympathy. Nonetheless, our instructions are clear."

"Do I understand that I have the perfect right to accept this situation and go back to my old job as it was under General Bottando?"

"You do. In theory."

"And in practice?"

In reply she received only a look. A very informative look.

"It is rare, I think, for people to find a new regime as comfortable as the one they were used to. The new head of department may not consider you to be so very obviously his deputy in the same way that General Bottando did. Indeed, he may well bring in his own people so that you revert to your official job as a researcher. You must consider seriously whether you would find that acceptable."

True enough. Flavia had got used to a great deal of unofficial authority in the past few years, as well as a considerable amount of independence. It would be very hard to lose that.

"You do realize," Flavia said, "the level of compensation and publicity I would receive if I took this to court? Dismissing a senior civil servant, which I am whether you like it or not, merely because she is expecting a baby . . ."

This was one detail that caught them on the hop. They both looked at her as though she had announced that she was the pope's daughter. Flavia could almost hear their strategy crumbling.

"Oh."

She smiled. "Against the law, you know. Even worse, it looks bad. It looks terrible."

"Well . . ."

"Tiresome, isn't it?" she said sympathetically. "Damned women, eh?"

"Naturally, we offer you our best congratulations."

"Thank you," she said. "And I'm sure you realize that, in the circumstances, a slight rethink of your position is necessary. Not to be crude about it, you want to ease me out quietly. Instead, what you will get is a public brawl. You might think it advisable to reconsider your offer—kind though it was."

She smiled. Even in her state of tiredness and shock she derived some considerable pleasure from their discomfort. Not that she believed for a moment she had won. It had been a skirmish, no more, but great victories are merely an accumulation of lots of little triumphs; you have to start somewhere. She had gained a little time to fight back, Flavia thought as she left the building and walked back to her car.

But still, she had little relish for the fight. She wanted the job, had worked for it, was good at it, and deserved it. It had been her life for twelve years. And yet, all of a sudden, she felt detached from it. Instead of the job being part of her, it was now something she did. With a shock of comprehension, she realized she was discontented with the routine, with her colleagues, with having to get up every morning and read reports on thefts she would never solve. She was fed up with keeping people happy, and battling constantly for a mere fraction of the money she needed. She was sick to death of maneuvering her way around people like those two characters. She had fought back out of principle, she realized, no more. She would not be treated like that. But her heart wasn't in it.

It was not just the two civil servants, she realized, who were going to have to reconsider their position.

*　　*　　*

One phrase that did stick in her mind was the crack about adhering to policy. Whatever that meant. In fact, the only policy she had not adhered to in recent months was the order to lay off the subject of Claude Lorrain. But why would anyone get so agitated about that? All she was trying to do was tidy up loose ends, keep the lid on. She should have been thanked, surely, rather than dismissed?

First things first, and that was to summon all those who might be interested and tell them everything that had been going on. Warts and all. They wanted a fight, they were going to get one, and the best way to start was to ensure that so many people knew about the whole Claude affair that there would be no more point in squashing her to keep it quiet. A secret shared is a secret defanged; another dictum of Bottando's.

She thought she would start with three people: Paolo, who wanted her job anyway and might now get it; Corrado, the trainee; and Giulia, the head researcher. No one else was around at the moment.

"My involvement," she concluded after a while, "seems to have been the cause of the decision to uproot me. I am not meant to be looking any further into this; why not I do not know."

"But it's only a picture," said Paolo, who always maintained the attitude that merely looking for stolen works of art, while entertaining, was a little beneath his ability. He still had a hankering after murder.

She shrugged. "True. But it is one connected to the powerful and influential."

Paolo stretched himself. "Well, now," he said lazily, "we will need all the dossiers we can lay our hands on here. On this Sabbatini, on his illustrious and dangerously powerful brother-in law. Ex-brother-in-law. Find Sabbatini's partners in crime of a decade or two ago, get the dossiers on them as well. Which just goes to prove how useful it is to do people favors. I know just the man. I'll give him a ring later on and twist an arm or two. Let's see if we can find out what all this is about, shall we? Don't pack your bags yet, eh?"

Flavia looked at him warmly. Considering that it would be very much in his own interests to sit tight and not lift a finger to help, she appreciated the gesture even more; a brief flicker of acknowledgment, and a slight shrug was his reply. Of course I want your job, it said, but not like this.

"Could you try and get phone records as well? For this journalist Dossoni as well, if possible. I'd like to know who's feeding him information. It might be a good idea to feed him a little more one day."

Everyone smiled happily at the prospect. There are few things quite as satisfying as leaking confidential information and seeing it turn up in the papers the next day.

"One more thing," Flavia continued. "There must be a report on the murder of Di Lanna's wife somewhere. Not letting the press know is one thing, but there had to be some sort of official investigation. That might be worth looking at."

They filed out, and Flavia sat for a while and looked around at her office, the bright sunny one that she had inherited from Bottando scarcely a year before. She wondered how much longer it would be hers.

She met Ettore Dossoni in a grubby little bar way past the Olympic stadium, and they went for a walk around it when the conversation finally got serious. The out-of-the-way meeting was Dossoni's idea when she'd phoned him; he disliked the idea of being close to people when talking about matters of importance. Over the years he had learned caution, he added, as well as respect for what electronic gadgetry could do. A windswept stadium would make even the most sophisticated device hard to operate, and they could guarantee being many meters away from anyone. It seemed excessively self-important to Flavia, but she was prepared to humor him.

So they walked past the grim limestone statues of Mussolini's ideal men time and again, while Flavia tried to do business with him. There was not a great deal she could offer in return, this was the problem. Just a chance for him to see whatever she might find, if she considered it appropriate.

Dossoni was a fat man who somehow hadn't realized that he was no longer young, lithe, and athletic. It gave him a strangely boyish way of walking, a loping stride that made his cheeks wobble, and the sweat stand out on a neck half strangled by a collar that had ceased to fit half a decade previously.

"So?" he said, after they'd walked for a while. "Are you going to threaten me with dire consequences if I don't reveal my sources?"

"No."

"What do you want?"

"You knew Maurizio Sabbatini, didn't you?"

"That," he said, "is probably in a file somewhere. So it would be foolish to deny it."

"Did you have as low an opinion of him as everyone else?"

Dossoni thought, then shook his head. "No, I didn't. Oddly enough, I think I had quite a high opinion of him."

"Why?"

"Because he was no fool. Unlike all the others. Think about it. There we were, a couple of hundred, maybe a couple of thousand students, earnestly discussing what we would do once we had overthrown world capitalism. Maurizio was the one at the back who would crease up with laughter and point out that perhaps, maybe, it wasn't going to be quite that easy, and that the most we could manage—if we were lucky—would be to make it look faintly ridiculous. We strutted about discussing revolution, he played his little jokes. None of us accomplished anything, the only difference was that he didn't expect to. He laughed at everybody."

"And then stopped laughing."

Dossoni nodded. "Ah, yes. You know about that, do you? I suppose you would."

"He disappears into bohemian semirespectability for nearly twenty years, then all of a sudden bursts into life with a grand stunt. You were meant to provide him with the publicity, weren't you?"

Dossoni thought carefully, then nodded. "I think that was his idea, yes. He said he was going to cause a huge embarrassment, just as in the past. Bigger, in fact. He was going to expose the hypocrisy of the state—fa la la. I had a great affection for him, but his language had scarcely changed in two decades. He still sounded like a pamphlet; more, perhaps, than he had back then."

"But nothing appeared in print. Why not?"

"I was waiting for some solid evidence he'd done something and that his story wasn't all hot air. He told me he'd pinched a picture; I rang you up and you said you knew nothing about it. Quite a plausible liar you are, as well."

"Thank you. I practice."

"Then he rang again and said that if I would get him an audience at the Janiculum on Friday I'd have the story of my life."

"Did you have any idea what he meant?"

"No. Still don't. He wanted lots of people near that great big statue of Garibaldi's wife. You know the one? The woman on the horse looking over the city. He didn't specify what the audience was going to be watching. I told him of course I wasn't going to do a damned thing for him unless he told me what he was up to. He said he couldn't, it was too dangerous. But he had all the pieces to set off an explosion that would shake the country to its foundation. Just trust him."

Dossoni paused and shook his head. "Trust him! Ha! I told him he had to be joking and I wouldn't trust him even if my job didn't depend on it. Then he rang off. Slammed the phone down, presumably. Except that I think it was a mobile phone. How do you slam down a mobile phone? Angrily pressing the off button isn't as expressive, really."

"I don't know. I've never thought about it. Then what?"

Dossoni shook his head. "Then nothing. The next I hear, he's found in his vat of plaster. I assumed it was all some sort of hoax that had failed and he'd got drunk in disappointment. I must say I was heartily relieved I'd had the common sense to have nothing to do with it."

Dossoni's story was not much, to be sure. Hardly worth bothering about. Deliberately or not, Dossoni had told her virtually nothing of interest. And now he was pushing her to say what she knew.

Well, why not? She was no longer in the business of keeping other people's secrets.

"Okay, then. This is the summary. Picture stolen. I hand over a ransom five days later and get it back . . ."

"How?"

"Direct exchange. With a man thought at the time to be Sabbatini, wearing a silly mask."

"Who was not Sabbatini."

"So it seems."

"Curious," Dossoni said. "Most curious."

"Do you know someone called Elena Fortini?"

Dossoni gave what seemed almost a shudder. Flavia looked at him inquiringly.

"Do *you* know her?" he asked back.

"Yes. I met her a couple of days ago."

"And your impressions?"

"I quite liked her. She seemed . . . sensitive, kind."

Dossoni threw back his head and laughed. "No wonder so few paintings are ever recovered," he said, "if the police are so perceptive."

"I beg your pardon?"

"I have heard Elena called many things, but not sensitive or kind," he went on. "Cruel, brutal. Not sensitive."

"She didn't strike me like that."

"She is the most violent person I have ever met," he went on. "An example. When one of her comrades was arrested on Good Friday, she suggested the appropriate response would be to bomb Saint Peter's during High Mass on Easter Sunday. Someone pointed out that hundreds of people might die, and she said, how appropriate. Christian sacrifice. The more the better. She was always into symbolic gestures. The symbol of the act. Remember that phrase? She was a great advocate of nail bombs. You know, the ones that tear off people's legs."

"None of this is in her file."

"She was wonderful at keeping in the background. And people were much too frightened of her to say anything, even when they were picked up. She was very much cleverer than anyone else. Poor old Maurizio was her puppet; she designed all his little actions for him; he was quite incapable of doing anything himself. But with her in charge everything had so many hidden messages it became surreal. She was an artist in violence. No one else could touch her. Did you ever see any of Maurizio's art, so-called, in the last few years?"

"Some. In his studio."

"Not very good, is it?"

"No."

"Confused, clumsy, incoherent. It was all he could manage, poor soul."

"Stealing this picture was a return to form, then," Flavia commented. "Very straightforward, that."

"Yes, but what does it mean? What's the interpretation, eh? That was the trouble with him. At the crucial juncture he became incoherent, meaningless. No intellectual depth, and what there was was supplied by Elena Fortini; she was much better educated, much smarter."

Unlike Dossoni, Flavia did not find the atmosphere of the Olympic stadium agreeable, or conducive to thought. Instead she went for a long walk.

Normally she did this with Argyll; they had spent years pounding the streets and hills of Rome together, amiably and in companionable harmony. Such jaunts were infinitely refreshing, but not the sort of thing that aids concentration. Argyll's boundless enthusiasm for bits of ancient Roman masonry sticking out from walls, or crumbling statues or patterns in cobblestones, was too distracting for that. He was forever shooting off with a gurgle of pleasure to look more closely at something or other, coming back when his curiosity was sated to pick up the conversation where it had been abruptly abandoned. "Oh, look, isn't that lovely," he was always saying, pointing out to Flavia something she might have passed a dozen times before without noticing.

But this day she had no appetite for architecture or sculpture or the oddities of town planning. She paced the streets, hands in the pockets of her jacket, frown on her face, eyes down, walking quickly across the town, over the river, and up the hill called the Janiculum to the statue of Garibaldi's wife on her horse in all her grandeur. To where the body of Maria di Lanna had been found nearly two decades ago, and where Sabbatini had told the journalist he wanted to stage his coup that would shake—what, exactly? There she sat for an hour thinking about the symbolism of Sabbatini's act. The phrase so enthusiastically taken up and put into action by the likes of Sabbatini. Odd how it had such an old-fashioned sound to it now, like some dead and buried artistic fad.

She began by trying to fit all the events into some pattern, but when that didn't work she tried it the other way around, constructing a pattern and seeing what events might fit in.

Some bits were easy; the date, in particular. Sabbatini had stolen the picture on Monday, then done nothing. Now she knew he had something planned for Friday, May 25. On May 25, 1981, his sister had been killed. Her body had been dumped close to where Flavia was now sitting, and that was where Sabbatini had wanted the cameras and audience to assemble, prompted by a reluctant Dossoni.

So far, so good. But why *that* picture? Any reason, or was that where Sabbatini's limited intellect let him down, as Dossoni had hinted? It was hard to see how a landscape by Claude could possibly have any hidden significance. Cephalus and Procris. The story even had a happy ending. Maybe he simply wanted a high-profile picture, stolen in a way that advertised what he was doing. Perhaps that was all there was to it.

But what was the point? A grand gesture to show to a bunch of old terrorists that he had not forgotten? How did that fit in his claim to Dossoni that he would shake the country to its foundations? Then there was the ransom demand. How did that fit in? Were there two messages? Or maybe whatever Sabbatini intended was abandoned when he died and his associate—and Flavia had not ruled out the possibility that Dossoni was three million dollars richer now than he had been last week—decided to cut his losses and collect the money.

Flavia sat on the bench next to Mrs. Garibaldi, reached for a cigarette, lit it, then pulled it out of her mouth and trampled on it. Oh, God, she thought. Can't even do that anymore. And, she suddenly realized, she was deliriously happy, and burst into tears.

All the tourists—not that there were many—looked on sympathetically.

"I tried to find that report on the Di Lanna kidnapping you asked for," Paolo said later when the four met in a restaurant to have dinner and discuss progress so far. He had begun by handing over a file of phone records, together with the apologetic remark that he hadn't had time to go through them. Not surprising. No one liked doing that. "No luck, alas. A curious story, though from what I have been able to gather. With a recent end."

"Yes?"

"As you said, it was all hushed up. Or, rather, it seems to have become one of those stories that everybody knew, but no one ever mentioned in public. Nevertheless, some aspiring and trouble-making magistrate did decide to investigate, and began working on the case. Unfortunately, it was for the wrong reasons; he seems to have had leftish sympathies and was more intent on causing trouble than establishing what happened. He was told to lay off and was then investigated himself; turns out he was as corrupt as you can get and still have only two legs. Eventually, to avoid the embarrassment of acknowledging dirty dealings in the judiciary, they cut him a deal. He resigns and is left in peace. End of story."

Flavia smiled. "Thank you. What's the recent end?"

"A few months ago. The magistrate dies."

"Suddenly?"

Paolo shook his head. "No. He'd been ill for some time, I think. Kidney gave up some time ago, had a transplant a year ago, and it didn't work. No surprise at all. Nothing suspicious, if that's what you were thinking."

She frowned. "I still can't figure any of this out," she said eventually. "Let us assume this Dossoni is right, and this is Elena Fortini and the symbolism of the act all over again. Let us assume that there is a connection between the Claude and the death of Maria di Lanna. What's the symbol? What was he trying to prove? And why now?"

She looked around the table. Blank faces. "Come on," she said. "Suggestions?"

Still silence.

"Anything?" she prompted.

Another silence.

Flavia sighed. "Well, thank you, anyway. That's very helpful. Nice to know you're all on form."

They finished their meal, talking of more tractable office problems. Paolo walked her home, which was kind of him, although he really wanted a private talk with her.

"We had a visit this afternoon," he said. "While you were out. Dour little fellow, from intelligence, he said. He walked straight in, straight into your office, and spent an hour going through your papers and files. I kept an eye on him as much as possible, and he didn't seem to find anything that he wanted."

Flavia couldn't think of anything to say.

"You seem to have upset some important people in some way," he continued thoughtfully. "If they want to send the spooks in, it might be reasonable to assume they haven't finished with you yet."

"Nothing I can do about it."

"Probably not. But if you are determined to continue with this business, you should at least take sensible precautions."

"Such as?"

"Such as not going home," he said as they turned the corner into the little square in front of Flavia's block and he gently pulled her back into the shadows. "After all, there is a spook car outside your door."

"How do you know?"

"Color, make, number plate, and little aerial sticking out the back. I have studied these things, you know. I once toyed with the idea of applying to be transferred there."

"And you didn't?"

"No. I did an interview. I've never come across such half-wits in my life. They wouldn't survive a week in the police. The point is, there they are, watching you."

"And I have to go home to find Jonathan."

"Ring." He pulled out his phone, dialed, and handed it to her. She listened to it chirrup away, and could faintly hear the telephone on the table in her bedroom also ringing in response. Just to the right of the little message Argyll had left her to say he was going to Tuscany for a day or so. The phone rang and rang, but no light was switched on, no friendly voice at the other end. Flavia didn't know whether to be irritated or glad.

"He doesn't have a phone, I suppose?" Paolo asked.

Flavia snorted. "If he had, you could be certain the batteries would be flat."

She scratched her head, and thought. "No, you're right. I'll go and find a hotel for the night."

Paolo offered to put her up, an offer Flavia refused, having met his children on too many occasions and knowing full well how little sleep she would get in a small apartment with screaming infants. She had, it seemed, only a few months of peace left to her. She did not want to waste a single night of them.

Half an hour later, rather than fretting about the security services or Maurizio Sabbatini, she drifted off to sleep in a little room on the Piazza Farnese worrying about the general smallness of Roman living space.

She had reasoned that, if anyone was looking for her, wanting to keep an eye on her movements, the last place they would think of looking would be a nunnery, and so, to a nunnery she had gone. The order of St. Bridget of Sweden has a very agreeable convent on the Piazza Farnese, part of it converted into a bed-and-breakfast hostel after their numbers went down. For the price it is exemplary, the nuns sweet, the location near perfect, and they already knew Flavia quite well; on a couple of occasions in the past she had put witnesses there where they would not be noticed. Several had come back for holidays when their troubles were over, while one went completely overboard, joined the order, and was last heard of doing good works in Burkina Faso.

As she ate her breakfast, simple but fresh, she worked her way through the files and press cuttings that Paolo had provided the previous evening, then distracted herself from the ever-present craving for a cigarette by writing down notes and thinking.

After a long period of staring into space, she realized why she was finding the whole business frustrating. She had concentrated on the symbolism of the act until it became clear that the case consisted of two parts, incompatible with each other.

Sabbatini steals the picture, then makes some sort of dramatic gesture in the Janiculum on Friday, May 25, to draw attention to the matter of his murdered sister. All clear and straightforward.

The second part, however, was the ransom. This would have been a better parallel, in fact. He could have contrasted the way pictures are rescued, but human beings are not. But Sabbatini had not demanded the ransom.

Let us concentrate on the Janiculum, she thought, buttering another roll. Friday—the television cameras arrive, a little bit of an audience, then Sabbatini makes his entrance. What then? Presumably some outrageous gesture. But, so what? Everybody says, How shocking or how funny, depending on what he does. Sabbatini is arrested and bundled off. What good does that do?

So, there must be something else. Elena Fortini, perhaps. Here she frowned, puzzled by the enormous difference between her own impression of the woman, and what the fat journalist had said. Could she be that far out? She had known some charming crooks in her time, that was certain. But Dossoni described her as being gratuitously cruel and violent. Did that really fit with the air of domesticity she had felt so strongly? Do cruel people make bread? Vicious ones iron their children's clothes?

And then there was Dossoni, who had intruded himself into this business quite uninvited. An old radical who had gone into journalism, like so many others and put his past behind him. An effortless switch in direction. Why not? Nothing suspicious there, even sensible to keep up old acquaintances, just in case they become interesting again. But there was no file on him. Why not? The Italian state kept files on everybody from those days, and most were perfectly easy to get at if you asked the right people. Paolo had drawn information on Sabbatini, on Fortini, even on Di Lanna, with no one raising an eyebrow. Yet there was no information on Dossoni. That was curious.

Ordinarily, the next step would have been simple; she would have picked up the phone and asked questions. Now she was reluctant to advertise her interest. So she had to fall back on other sources, and had to think hard before she came up with one that might work. Then she finished her coffee—was she even allowed coffee anymore? She'd have to check. And come to think of it, weren't her feet a little swollen? She told the nuns she would stay another night if they had room, and walked out into the bright morning sunlight to head for the Vatican.

It took a long time to get in; even had she been willing to advertise herself by using her police identity card, the Vatican is normally quite sniffy about admitting Italian officials. It does so eventually, of course, but it is an independent state and goes through the motions of guarding its privileges jealously. So Flavia had to present herself at the main door as a private visitor, then wait in a rundown and dingy room for nearly forty minutes before Aldo Morante bounced in and gave her a most unpriestly kiss.

She had never quite mastered the ability to keep a straight face whenever she thought of Father Aldo Morante. Even after a decade or more, he still looked like an actor pretending to be a priest, and not succeeding very well. He was just too big for the part, too exuberant, too noisy, and too obviously had trouble with the vows of chastity to be entirely convincing. A priest he was, nonetheless, having converted straight from communism to Catholicism some fifteen years back without the usual progression through disenchantment, skepticism, and conversion. Why waste time? he'd once said to her. We'll all end up on our knees again one day. Might as well get on with it now, keep ahead of the field.

Once upon a time, however, he'd been a firebrand of radicalism, no meeting left unattended, no pamphlet left unread, and all speeches delivered at the top of his voice, preferably with a megaphone. Even though he was a decade older than she was, Flavia knew him because their mothers were friends and he had always had a benevolent affection for her, which even survived her entering the police. Her total lack of interest in politics was forgiven her, as family and connections have always, quite rightly, been considered of far more importance than transitory ideologies. So Flavia had watched Aldo metamorphose over the years from youthful choirboy, through political revolutionary, and around again to earnest churchgoer. She had kept a distant eye on him as he started life in a parish, found the work tedious, then worked his way into a job at the Vatican where he was now an ambitious undersecretary of some small importance in the Church's equivalent of the foreign ministry.

Slight ostentation had always been his trademark, so Flavia knew perfectly well that when he escorted her to his office by putting his arm around her waist it was purely and simply so that the people in the corridors who passed them would notice. For all the playacting, however, he was someone who had never wasted time with chatter.

"What do you want, then?" he said, the moment the door of the little office was closed.

"Help. Urgently," she replied. There is nothing like childhood to relieve you of the necessity for diplomacy.

"Go on, then. Let's have it."

So he got it; from the theft of the Claude, right through to the security men camped outside her door.

"Now," he said when she'd finished, "if I read you correctly, you suspect Ettore Dossoni of horrendous duplicity simply because this other woman spotted you were going to have a baby before you knew yourself."

Flavia opened her mouth to make a sharp reply, then considered. "That's partly right," she said after a brief hesitation. "I suppose. Also because he said that he talked to Sabbatini on the phone and none of Sabbatini's phone records show any signs of it. I checked this morning. Not that that is proof, of course."

"Congratulations, by the way," Aldo went on. "You'll be a very good mother. I trust it will be the first of at least half a dozen. I will baptize them all myself. I need a bit of practice. Now, Dossoni. I remember him. There was always a bit of a smell about him, if you see what I mean."

"There still is."

"I don't mean his hygiene; that was fashionable. Everybody smelled. You were just too naive to realize that deodorant was a capitalist plot. I mean, there was always a whiff of something slightly unsavory about Dossoni. Everybody had their doubts where he was concerned."

"Meaning?"

"Now, you're expecting me to speak ill of people. Which I cannot do, being a priest, and having to think worthy thoughts all the time. So, I'll get the book on him."

"What book?"

"This is the Vatican, child. We know everything. You must remember, the Church was in cahoots with the government back then, and our foreign intelligence was second to none. We swapped what we knew about foreign lands with what the Italian government knew about goings on here. There, I should say. And annotated what we were given with our own sources."

"Can you get hold of this stuff?"

"I am a senior official, you know. Should be monsignor by next year."

"Congratulations."

"Hmm. Fancy a red hat, though. Crimson has always suited me. Now, I can't of course show you the files themselves; they are terribly confidential. What I will do is read them and answer questions about them. Silly, I know, but there we are. Rules are rules. Why don't you look at some pictures while you wait. It might take some time."

"I've seen them," Flavia said crossly. "Many times."

Aldo waved a hand. "Oh," he said, "not *those* pictures; I didn't mean the museum. I mean the good ones; the ones the public doesn't see."

And to keep her occupied while he hunted, Aldo led Flavia through back corridors into rooms that looked older and older, until he came to a door. "Through there," he said. "Off you go. I'll come and get you when I'm done."

He wafted off and Flavia thought idly how curious it would be to see Aldo as a cardinal. And why stop there? How would he look in white? Then she opened the door and forgot such trivia. She spent the next hour looking openmouthed at a collection of paintings that made the Vatican Museum itself look second-rate.

It is amazing how fast time passes when you are astonished; the only conscious thought Flavia had in the entire period was that she wished Argyll had been there, although he would have been in such a delirium it might have been days before she got a coherent remark from him.

And she especially wanted Argyll there when she came to one particular picture. It was a Dormition, the last sleep of the Virgin. She wasn't as good as Argyll, nowhere near, but she knew the picture; or rather, she knew a face. It was the same face as the one in the Madonna above Bottando's fireplace. Same size panel, more or less, same reds in the clothing. She was no expert, couldn't swear to anything, but under Argyll's tutelage she had spent a long time looking at pictures as well as looking for them. And this one was just too similar. Must have been part of a triptych, the only difference being this one still had a proper frame, complete with the little iron hinges that would have linked it to the bigger, central panel. That, presumably, would have been another scene from the life of the Virgin. But what was it? She looked, but there was no notice, no useful little plaque. Damnation. She began to understand how Argyll felt.

"Enjoy it?" Aldo remarked as he breezed back in, although whether it was an hour or two later Flavia could not tell. "I thought you might."

"What's this?" she asked, pointing at the little panel.

He shrugged. "No idea. Not my area. I do foreign policy, not pictures."

"Who does know?"

He shrugged without any interest at all.

"Where did these come from?" she asked.

He shrugged once more. "Oh, here and there. And most should not, strictly speaking, be here. That's why they're kept hidden."

"What does that mean?"

Aldo began to look embarrassed. "I'm beginning to regret showing you these. In fact, I shouldn't have. So don't ask anymore. Now, business," he said briskly, dismissing the matter and refusing to let Flavia interrupt. "Here we are. Now you can ask away and I will answer with all the omniscience of someone who has read the files while you have not."

Flavia tried to remember why she had come in the first place, and dragged her eyes away from the little panel. "Dossoni?" she asked, giving way reluctantly.

"I now remember him very well. He was a narc."

"Really?"

"Yup. Two-faced, double-dealing police informer, if he wasn't worse. He knew far too many of the wrong sorts of people and probably still does."

Flavia shook her head, and thought about this while Aldo paced up and down and looked with bored indifference at a painting or two. He'd always been a bit of a philistine in this department, Flavia thought.

"And all this would have been in the file my colleague couldn't get hold of? No wonder it was restricted. What about the Di Lanna kidnapping itself? Was there a file on that?"

"A very big one. Most of it you will know; there seems to have been little new, except for noting the fact that Di Lanna, when he got control of the money, poured funds into the Christian Democrats, and used it to try and wrest control of Bologna from the communists. And, I assume, feathered the nests of many politicians at the same time. Our beloved prime minister grew surprisingly rich in those years, but then gratitude is a wonderful thing, and he does genuinely seem to have done his best."

"What about this magistrate and his report on the murder?"

"Very little. We don't have much on that at all. Only newspaper cuttings."

"Anything else?"

"That's it. What's the matter? You look disappointed."

"I was hoping for something a bit more substantial."

The future monsignor looked disapproving. "I've done the best I can. What do you expect? Miracles? The Vatican isn't really the place to come to for that sort of thing, you know."

And where was Jonathan Argyll? Flavia thought to herself as she lumbered slowly on a bus full of excited tourists into the center of the city. How on earth could he disappear just when he was needed? She relied on him at moments such as these to sit and listen and make remarks, some useless, some perceptive, but always helping her think and explain and work through whatever was going on in her mind. Without him around she felt she wasn't as clearheaded as she needed to be, and no one else she knew came even remotely close to being able to stimulate her powers of reason. The nearest, perhaps, was Bottando, but he was a distant second.

But there it was. The phone at home still went unanswered; she even tried Bottando but he had also vanished off the face of the

earth. She had been, in effect, abandoned at one of the most important moments of her life by the two people she really relied on. It
was enough to make the most sensible person feel resentful. And
after five minutes thinking about it, Flavia did feel resentful, so she
picked on a spotty adolescent sitting down minding his own business and harming no one.

"No one ever tell you to get up for pregnant women?" she
barked in a motherly tone.

He looked up at her in alarm.

"Go on," she said, "up you get," and watched with mild satisfaction as he blushed shamefacedly and reluctantly moved away,
muttering darkly.

"Thank you, young man," she said brightly, and sat down herself. That was the good thing about Italy, she thought. Maternal
authority still had a bit of bite in it.

Now then, she thought as she settled down and slipped a shoe
off so she could massage her toes, Dossoni. Radical-cum-informer-
cum-journalist. Which presumably Maurizio Sabbatini did not
know, otherwise he would not have involved him . . .

But Aldo had said everyone knew, and despite his manner he
chose his words carefully. The implications of this sank in slowly as
she worked on her big toe. Would Sabbatini be so stupid as to bring
in someone he thought might well be a police informer, if not
worse? Surely not. Therefore, Dossoni's source of information on
the theft could not have been Sabbatini. And she wasn't it either.
And she doubted that it was the director of the museum. And there
was only one other place the information could have come from.

And any further thoughts stopped dead. The bus had arrived at
her stop, and she found for some reason that she couldn't get her
shoe back on. At least the sight of her hopping to the door gave
the pimply youth some small satisfaction.

16

Age had withered her somewhat, but what remained was still decidedly handsome. Mary Verney had the sort of face that improved as it settled into an age that revealed more of the bones. She was as oddly dressed as she often was, with what looked very much like a drying-up cloth wrapped around her head to fend off the sun, but such eccentricities were for private moments; when on display she could be remarkably elegant.

She also had the charm and manners that come from years of practice, although, it seemed, surprise could occasionally put even this well-honed instrument under some strain. She was not expecting a visitor. When Argyll finally gave up postponing and presented himself at her house an hour later, the welcome was not as wholehearted as it might have been had she been given a few moments' notice.

Even so, she did quite well, enthusiastically presenting both cheeks for a peck, chirruping about delightful surprises, how pleased she was, do come and sit down. The matter taken out of his hands, Argyll smiled, and let himself be led up the four worn steps to the terrace, forward toward the table, and then introduced to the guest. Not that any introduction was needed.

"Good afternoon, Jonathan," said Taddeo Bottando, rising to

his feet to greet him. "I'm most surprised to see you here. What can we do for you?"

"Just passing. Thought I'd drop in," he said, then smiled foolishly. "No. In fact, I came to ask you about a painting," he said, thinking that in the circumstances dithering and polite talk really ought to be dispensed with. "You're the only people who can help."

A good start, which he then went and spoiled with delaying tactics. "I tracked you down, you see, and was in the area. Just down the road, in fact. I had lunch in that little restaurant in the square. Very agreeable. And saw the church. Have you seen the church? The altarpiece? Liked it enormously."

"Many times," Mary Verney said patiently. "Are you here on your own?"

"Oh yes."

"And where is your wife?"

"Flavia?" Argyll asked.

"You have more than one?"

"Oh no. Just the one. Quite enough, really. She's back in Rome. Trying to tidy up after this Claude business. Not very happy, I must say. A bit discouraged, in fact. Disillusioned, you know."

"Why is that?"

Argyll thought. "I don't know, really. She's been a bit off-color recently. Distracted. Grumbling. She has discovered what General Bottando has known for years, I suspect, that her superiors are almost as pernicious as the art thieves themselves. Just less straightforward."

"I did mention it to her," Bottando said with a faint smile.

"But you rather protected her from the direct experience," Argyll commented. "And she's just coming round to realizing how grateful she was. But your going, and the way you went, removed the last illusions. That and the Claude thing, of course. She's more fed up than I've ever seen her."

Bottando looked sad for her.

Argyll went on, reinvigorated now that that part of the conversation was disposed of. "This painting I want to ask you about."

Mary Verney poured him a glass of wine, and smiled encouragingly. He drank. In fact, he thought, he'd had quite a few of these today. The heat didn't help either.

"And a crime," he added, in order to make them more comfortable, to bring both back into a world with which they were all too familiar. The comment did not succeed, however; rather they just sat there, side by side. Had Argyll been less in turmoil, he would have found it touching. And would have been glad for both of them, that they could take such comfort from, and pleasure in, each other's company.

For they were a perfect match, if you looked at it elliptically and disregarded all the practical details of why they shouldn't even be talking to each other. Like the fact that Mary Verney had spent her life stealing pictures, and Taddeo Bottando had spent his trying to get them back again. Both were kindly, intelligent, with, as far as Argyll knew, many of the same interests, even if they did approach them somewhat differently. Both (Flavia had long suspected, as she was given to speculating on such matters) were desperately lonely, and growing more so as the years went by.

This train of thought had made him drift off a little, while the other two sat there patiently, waiting for him to get his bearings.

"Now, then," he resumed with an attempt at decisiveness. "This painting. And theft . . ."

"Do get on with it, Jonathan," said Mary Verney a little tartly. "I know you like to affect absentmindedness, but you really are overdoing it a little. Say what you've come to say. Then do whatever you've come to do."

Argyll peered at her, wondering whether to take offense, and decided she was probably right. "Very well, then," he said. "Buonaterra. Nineteen sixty-two."

The look of surprise on both their faces was carefully controlled, but just enough sneaked through for Argyll to realize that all the connections he'd been making were correct. So he went on.

"A perfect crime," he said. "Or very nearly. That is, a crime hidden inside another one. But it is the point of it, and the ending of it, that confuses me. That's why I'm here.

"So, the events. Someone steals a painting for reasons that have nothing to do with money, and hides it. Then Mary Verney comes along and steals it from the thief. The first bit I know; the second bit I guess. Perfect cover. The thief can't complain, and the police are hardly likely to connect you with the matter. After all, you weren't around when the original theft was committed. You were here.

"Now, the matter that confuses me was that the picture was then returned to its owner. Considering that the person who took it was, by then, well into her career as a professional thief, and that she was perfectly in the clear, this is the bit that doesn't make a great deal of sense.

"If," he went on vaguely, "there was a ransom paid for it—a big ransom—then I could see the point of giving it back. Much better to have the cash and not have to worry about getting rid of the picture, which is always the tricky bit, so I understand. But there was no ransom. So it doesn't make sense, you see."

Not a very impressive performance, in Argyll's opinion. He'd imagined himself delivering a more incisive summary of the business, not the inchoate ramble that in fact had come from his mouth. No matter, it worked. What he said made the right impression; what he didn't say made an even bigger one.

It seemed that Bottando had ceded the lead role here to Mary Verney; he sat quietly and let her do the talking, perhaps because all his years as a policeman had made him better at asking questions than answering them. Or perhaps it was because it was her house.

"What's your interest in this picture, by the way?" she asked.

"It was meant to be a retirement present for the general here," he said sadly. "He'd always said it was valueless. I thought it might be worth something. Flavia said he was worried that retiring a little earlier than he'd anticipated would dent his pension, so I was going to present him with provenance, and all that stuff, so that if he wanted to sell it . . ."

"That was very kind of you."

"But then, of course, it all got wrapped up in other things. And raised lots of questions that have been nagging at me. I have established that it is quite possibly hugely valuable—important, anyway. Bulovius said so, just before he died. But I don't know what it is yet; I can't prove it, anyway, and I don't know exactly where you two fit in, although fit in you do."

"You're sure of that, are you?" she said, with a faint smile. "Well, then, I suppose you might as well know the rest, as well. Have some more wine."

"No. Thank you."

She shrugged, thought a minute, then began.

"I feel terribly sorry for the youth of today, I really do," she began. "Their lives are so cramped in comparison to ours. And everything is increasingly the same. Wherever you go, all you see are the same disgusting fast-food restaurants, which seems to have originated in Kansas and should never have been allowed to leave. When I was young, foreign lands were still foreign, life was terribly inexpensive, and jobs easy to get, if you were unfortunate enough to need one.

"And people were so very trusting; now if you even go into a church you're lucky if there is not a camera watching your every genuflection, just in case. I do believe that I had the great fortune to be young at the highest point that civilization has ever reached. It will just about see me out, but when I go I will not regret the pleasures my death will deny me. Well, maybe some, " she added with a sidelong look at Bottando.

"Anyway, from the end of the fifties until the end of the sixties, life was a delight. Age, combined with selective memory, make it seem better than it was, no doubt. But, in my opinion, it was a period of a few years where wealth had not yet brought tawdriness, freedom had yet to descend into self-indulgence, and the freshness of change was hopeful rather than a desperate search for repetitive novelty. And I, with no one to please but myself, was determined to make the most of it.

"And so I did. As you know all too well, I embarked on a career for which I was eminently suited, and ensured myself an income which was more than generous. But for all that, I was in every other way utterly respectable; what I really wanted, I think, was the sort of life that everyone else seemed to have. A husband who looked after me, two children, a nice house, preferably with roses growing up the outside. I was even prepared to consider coffee mornings with the girls. My rather disrupted childhood, no doubt, contributed to this desire of mine, and I put it into practice more or less at the first opportunity. I met Jack Verney and, although I knew quite well he was unsuitable in every way, I married him. He was a nice man. He was also the most boring man who has ever walked the face of the earth. I do him no injustice here; he said it himself, and was rather proud of his ability to make entire dinner parties fall asleep under the impact of yet another of his interminable golfing stories.

"He traveled a great deal, fortunately, leaving me to my own devices, and when he was off on one tour, I took the opportunity to go to Italy, where I bought this house. It cost me one hundred and fifty pounds—not much, even then—and I had this fond notion of spending time here, with my husband and children, when I had them. For the rest of the time, I set about supplementing my little Swiss nest egg.

"I was not what you might call truly operational at this stage, you understand. I had stolen one painting in my youth, on which I had made no money for myself, and followed up with a couple of others to keep body and soul together, but turned over a new leaf on my marriage. Then Ettore Finzi approached a dealer about a commission, and the dealer approached me. Would I, for a generous sum, steal a picture of an Immaculate Conception from the Stonehouse villa? It seemed he'd had a pair of pictures and considered he'd been cheated out of both of them. If I would recover the first, then he would also give me a substantial sum later to recover the second."

"Where's the second?"

She shrugged. "I don't know. We never got to the second. I was going to be in Italy anyway, and once I thought about it, it seemed an easy enough thing to do; private houses back then were so easy to rob that it was almost embarrassing. So I agreed, wangled an invitation to visit Buonaterra, and was all set.

"I may say, by the way, that I had no idea what the picture was. Still have no idea. Finzi was old and sick and terribly suspicious. All I got was a description of what I was to take. I knew, of course, that the rivalry between him and Stonehouse had been bubbling away for longer than anyone could remember, but I didn't really need to know more than that in any case.

"So I arrived, settled in, made myself useful, and began to prepare myself. Then that idiot Bulovius showed up and ruined everything. Not only did he spend much of his time chasing me round the rosebushes, so I scarcely had a moment on my own to blow my nose, let alone steal a painting, he then decides to show Finzi what a good boy he is. He had ingratiated himself with the old man in a quite disgusting fashion—I think he already had ideas about the will—and it occurred to him that bringing Finzi the picture would be just the sort of display of loyalty that would finally secure him his place in the list of beneficiaries. I don't suppose this was the interpretation he gave you, though.

"Anyway, I had everything set up. I'd figured out the way to get the picture out of the house—a runner was going to be waiting down the lane to take it off my hands so that I wouldn't have to hold it for more than a few minutes, another one was going to collect it from the left luggage at the railway station and get it out of the country. Everything was set; Stonehouse had invited me to dinner, and I would have needed about five minutes to leave the table, proceed to the room, go into the garden, hand over the picture, and be back for pudding. So I went home for the night and arrived the next day to discover the picture had already vanished, the police were everywhere, and Bulovius had this sickly green look of terrified guilt plastered all over his face. His behavior the next day was so laughable that it was hard to resist just asking him to hand it over.

"I was not concerned about the police very much; they did not seem likely to give me much serious competition. The man in charge —what was his name?

"Tarento," Bottando said, speaking about it for the first time.

"Tarento. Yes. He was a perfect fright, and quite the stupidest policeman I had ever met. But sweet and amiable in his way," she went on, demolishing part of Argyll's imaginary reconstruction, "and dreadfully kind to Taddeo here," she added, flattening another.

"So I didn't really think there was much to worry about from that direction. Which was a mistake, as while his superior lacked investigative drive and enthusiasm, Taddeo had both in abundance. And early on I saw him watching Bulovius with a level of interest that only flickering suspicion could arouse. So I took the trouble to engage him in conversation to try and get his measure. It was a bad mistake. Quite simply, I fell completely in love with him.

"Now, I am not a romantic soul—quite the opposite, in fact. I always believed myself immune from such feelings; this was why I married my husband, as I thought mild affection was more than enough. To fall in love so unexpectedly, so instantly, and with the most inappropriate person in the world simply took my breath away. It made me foolish in a way I have never been before. Even worse, Bottando was utterly unresponsive as far as I could see and, moreover, was taking far too close a professional interest in me. He watched me like a hawk; even had I been capable of coherent action, it would have been quite difficult to do anything. I had wild imaginings that there was a file on me, and that they had already earmarked me as the likely thief; that I was going to spend several years in jail for the one picture I didn't steal. The only thing I didn't remotely consider as a possibility was that I had had the same effect on him as he had on me. I had a high notion of my abilities, but I never thought of myself as someone people fell in love with.

"The worst moment was when I forced myself to go into Florence to have a meeting with the runner, to reschedule getting the picture out of Italy should I get hold of it. It was stupid—the one and only time I ever had direct dealings with such people. Fortunately, the man I had chosen was not well known. Otherwise seeing me come out of his apartment block would have been enough to make even the thickest policeman suspicious.

"And Bottando was not stupid, which was why, when I saw him standing across the street, looking at me when I emerged, I came as near to panic as I have ever done. Even worse, he wouldn't come to the point, just talked to me, said he was off duty, and would I care to go for a walk? It was the oddest interrogation I have ever been through because, I suppose, it wasn't one. Instead, we just walked. And walked and walked. We visited churches, and we visited museums and courtyards and byways and alleyways. You do the same with Flavia, I know you do. There is nothing better in the world than to share the pleasure of a little discovery, a new sight, or a new picture with someone. I had never felt so happy in anyone's company before in my life. I will not go into any further details, if you don't mind. I will merely say that we came back here to my little house, and spent a lovely weekend together.

"Except for the fact that he was a policeman. And that was a major stumbling block. I decided that he was warning me. We know about you, he was saying. Watch yourself.

"So I did. I was not about to pay the price of someone else's folly, thank you very much. It was a ticklish situation, as you can imagine. On the one hand, I wanted to get that picture; on the other, the risks were large, and I have always disliked risks.

"So I waited, and slowly became reassured. The police seemed to lose interest, everything went quiet. I had already figured out by watching Bulovius, and the way he got nervous every time someone sat on the sofa, where the picture was, and late one night, after I had spent an hour in the garden waiting for everyone to go to bed, I slipped back into the house, put it in a little bag, and walked out.

"Straight into the arms of Taddeo. He had been hiding nearly every night for days. Waiting for something to happen. It was a lovely night, with a beautiful moon, and I could see the look of vague amusement on his face. I was speechless, so he did the talking.

" 'Congratulations,' he said. 'You found it.'

"I said I had, and that I could explain.

" 'No need to. I know what happened. You were looking for an earring, peered under the settee, and there it was. So you picked it up and decided to take it yourself to the police station.'

"It seemed a perfectly reasonable explanation to me, so I nodded.

" 'It might be difficult, however,' he went on, 'to explain that to Mr. Stonehouse. He might ask why you were taking it out of the house at all. He might become angry about the whole business, and wonder whether in fact you took it in the first place.'

"I said it would be terribly unkind of him even to think such a thing.

" 'Maybe it would be better, if you were willing to forgo thanks for recovering the picture, if we didn't say how it was recovered? Perhaps if it was just found?'

"I agreed to the inevitable and we left it, wrapped in a bag for protection, in a ditch, where Bottando duly picked it up the next morning with me there as a witness, and handed it in to general applause. It was a terrible emotional wrench, but I left that same afternoon, went back to England, and steered clear of Italy for some time. When I started working again, it was a full decade before I took any commissions for Italy.

"But, for old time's sake, when I heard that the Stonehouse collection was to come up at auction, I looked in the catalog, saw the picture was there, and bought it. I sent it to Taddeo as a little keepsake—complete with the invoice so he wouldn't be concerned. I was glad to see he still had the picture when we met again. That meant a lot to me.

"Anyway, for more than thirty-five years I put Taddeo Bottando behind me and got on with my life, which was perfectly satisfactory until Flavia began investigating me and I met Taddeo again. Then I realized that some things simply cannot be put behind you. And as he let it be known that he felt exactly the same, we decided we were too old for any more delay. I was already in retirement, he decided to take his as soon as possible, and here we are. And here, I very much hope, we stay."

Bottando said nothing during this lengthy exposition; simply sat and looked benignly from one to the other, smiling occasionally, and sipping his drink. When Mary Verney finally finished, Argyll stared glumly at both of them. It was not what she had not mentioned that bothered him, it was the fact that, on what was in some ways the central point, she was clearly and obviously telling the truth. When he saw Bottando looking at her, he knew the expression well, and knew what feeling lay behind it. It was the way he looked at Flavia. He knew just enough about them to realize that both had led lives that had a deeply unhappy core, for both were naturally affectionate, and neither had had any proper object for their affection.

They had tasted it once, walking the streets of Florence, and now they were grabbing it with both hands and with a desperation only the truly deprived can manage. Was he going to spoil it for them? Was it really supposed to be his job to snatch it all away?

"Do you know," he said, staring hazily in the direction of the sun, which was beginning to sink behind some pine trees halfway up the next hill, "Flavia has always had a considerable admiration for you. Professionally, that is."

"I'm flattered to hear it."

"Hmm. She once told me that of all the thieves she had ever come across, you had one quality which set you apart from the others."

"And that was?"

"Discipline. Rigorous self-discipline. Most are caught, you see, because they become lazy—these are her words, not mine, you understand—so they repeat themselves. One particular way of stealing something works, so they do it again. And again. You were the only one to have infinite variety, beyond the fact, as the general here once noted, that none of the things you stole were photographed or, until recently, recovered."

"We all have our little trademarks."

"So it seems," he said, a little sadly.

17

The realization that she had told almost everything she knew to a man who, it seemed, was quite possibly still connected to the intelligence services made Flavia feel distinctly paranoid. So much so that when she got to her car—thanking heaven that she always kept the key in her pocket rather than leaving it in the apartment—she checked it carefully, inside and out, underneath and in the engine and around the petrol tank. Stranger and nastier things had happened.

But the car seemed fine, and she drove off quickly, following a roundabout route, up and down little alleyways, stopping frequently, doing illegal U-turns, driving the wrong way down one-way streets, just to make sure no one was taking an undue interest in where she was going. She kept up the routine when she got to the autostrada as well, although the suddenly uncooperative nature of her bladder and the fact that for the first time in her life she felt carsick meant that she had to stop frequently.

Again, nothing untoward appeared in her mirror, no one seemed to look at her with more attention than was warranted, and gradually she relaxed. It was three o'clock, after a long drive, made longer by the frequent stops, when she arrived once more in Siena. She parked in La Lizza, a part of the town that rarely appears on tourist postcards, considered for a moment whether she was doing the right thing, then walked into the school where Elena Fortini earned her living.

She had to wait; Elena was giving a class, and had another twenty minutes to go, so she sat, walked around, read the notice-board full of trips and offers of accommodation and old cars for sale, and finally stared out of the window wondering why time so often seemed to drag along so slowly. It was unlike most schools; no bell signaled the end of lessons, there was no sudden outburst of noise and movement as the pupils cascaded out of the classrooms. This was a serious place, mainly for students dissatisfied with the teaching at the university, or businessmen trying to show how keen they were to get on, or people who wanted jobs in the town's hotels and needed to be able to talk to the guests.

Very dull, little life. Flavia scarcely noticed any of it as she was lost in a particularly distant pattern of thoughts; only when Elena Fortini tapped her on the shoulder did she return to earth and turn round.

"They said I had a visitor," she began. "I'm glad you didn't say who you are."

"Can we go somewhere quiet?"

Elena shrugged. "Fine. Inside or out? It's a nice day. Let's go for a walk. If you're up to it."

She was, but only for about ten minutes, then she began to feel extraordinarily weary, so they went into a hotel Flavia had stayed in once before, many years ago, and ordered a bottle of cold water and coffee, and sat in a small cloister in the shade. It was almost too beautiful to talk of anything serious. So they didn't, for a while, but sat quietly together, with Flavia more and more convinced that her instincts were—must be—superior to any other evidence.

There was, though, only one way to find out. "I've been looking into you, and into Sabbatini," she said. "And getting conflicting reports. Like your being known in your past for excessive violence and cruelty. I was also told that Sabbatini never thought up his own stunts. They were always designed and planned by you, who stayed safely in the background. "I've also caught you out in a particular lie. You said you hadn't heard from Sabbatini in ten years. That wasn't true."

Elena smiled. "Can you prove it?"

"As near as I need to. He phoned your school in February. It's in his phone records."

"And how could you know that?" she said scornfully.

"You mean, how could I know when he used a public phone? Simple. Because he was an idiot and used a charge card to pay for it."

"Doesn't mean I spoke to him. Maybe I was teaching."

"That can be checked, no doubt."

"Or out for a coffee."

"The phone call lasted thirteen minutes. It doesn't take that long to be told you're not there."

"So I forgot. Sorry. It slipped my mind."

"Ettore Dossoni." Flavia noted the sudden caution in the woman's pose as she mentioned the name.

"What about him?"

"He's the one who says you are exceptionally violent and dangerous."

"If he's right, it's risky of you to tell me, then."

"He's now a journalist, and rang me up soon after the theft to make inquiries. He says Sabbatini tried to persuade him to publicize the whole thing. He also is lying."

"Very perceptive of you." She smiled. "No, I mean it. I'm not being entirely sarcastic. Go on, please."

"I'm fairly certain he got his information from somewhere in the government, at least. He was checking up on me, to make sure I was being as discreet as instructed. He was working for the security services twenty years ago, and probably still is in some form. A couple of hours after I talked to him, someone put a car outside my apartment, which worries me."

"So it should," she said, suddenly serious.

"Why?"

"Go on talking to me. I might tell you later, depending on what you say."

"As far as I know it now, the events went like this: Sabbatini steals the picture on Monday, and plans some grand coup for the following Friday, the anniversary of his sister's death. On Wednesday, a ransom demand arrives. Two days later I—or rather my colleague—hands over the ransom money down the Appian Way and recovers the picture. End of story. But."

Elena Fortini looked at her inquiringly.

"But who handed the picture back and took the money? There are two possibilities. One is Dossoni, the other is you."

She turned to see how this suggestion was received. It was not received very well. Elena Fortini took a sip of water, and shook her head.

"Wrong," she said simply. "Or at least, wrong in your conclusions about me. I can't comment on Dossoni, of course. However, all that evening I was teaching a long revision class that went on until past ten o'clock. The students had a big exam on Monday and needed a lot of help. I have twenty people to prove I was here. And if you think I could get from a classroom in Siena to the Appian Way in under two hours, you have a higher estimation of my poor old car than it deserves."

"I'm open to suggestions."

"And what would you do if I did tell you something of interest?"

"I don't know. My original intention was to tidy up loose ends and save everybody embarrassment. Like a good public servant. It seems to have got a bit beyond that. I thought I was dealing with a stolen picture. The picture seems only a small part of it now. Although part of what I do not know. But Sabbatini is dead, his sister was murdered, a large amount of money has gone missing. And no one wants me to look into it at all. I'd like to know why, and get people off my back."

"If that's the case then I won't tell you anything," Elena said. "I'm not going to break cover just to make you feel comfortable. It's too dangerous. And I'm not being melodramatic."

Flavia looked at her seriously. "Look, I could arrest you as an accessory. I won't—won't even threaten it. You can sit there, drink your coffee, say nothing, walk out. There will be no consequences, no reports, nothing. If you tell me what you know, if there is anything I can do about it, I will. But I must be honest; I doubt there is."

Elena rocked herself back and forth and thought. "So do I." She paused, then took a deep breath. "I kidnapped Maria di Lanna. Was that in your files?"

"No."

"Good. I was worried about Maurizio when he was arrested. Courage was not his strong point, and I knew that he would say anything to get himself out of trouble. We needed something to make sure he realized that he had to keep quiet. Kidnapping Maria was a message he could not fail to understand."

Flavia stopped herself from saying that shooting her in the head probably got through as well.

"So we took her, and held her. A nice woman, oddly. Desperately spoiled, of course, but no whiner. I liked her. She was upset and frightened, obviously, but we reassured her it was only for a week, then she calmed down. It was true, as well. We planned to hold her only for long enough for Maurizio to hear about it and get the message.

"The day before we planned to let her go, the police came. The army, whatever. I was out; Maria said she wanted some cornflakes, so I went to the shop to get them for her. I also bought her a little cake. With a candle. We were going to have a little party that evening to say good-bye. Can you believe it?" She shook her head. "I even bought some party hats.

"No party. I saw the cars draw up as I was coming out of the shop, so I watched from the distance. I heard the gunfire, saw the troops storm in, heard my comrades and friends being killed. Pop pop pop. They didn't even fire back; it was too much of a surprise. Five people in there, all killed within seconds." She paused. "You don't look very shocked."

"Should I be?"

"I suppose not. All that I want to say is that there was no attempt to arrest anybody. It was shoot to kill, no questions asked. We expected it in one way, but it was still a shock. A long time ago, and not important. What is important is that after all the shooting was over, I saw Maria. Alive and well, being bundled out of the house and into a waiting car."

"She was alive? She was rescued? Are you certain?

"Alive and unharmed. Believe me, I can never forget it; as she was being led to the car she looked across the road and saw me, clutching the cornflakes. I thought, Christ, she's going to point me out, and I got ready to run, but she didn't. Do you know what she did? She winked at me. She did nothing at all except wink at me. Then turned her head away, allowed herself to be put in the car, and was driven off."

She stopped, still remembering that faint smile, then shook her head and drummed on the marble-topped table with her fingers. Thick, short fingers, they were, Flavia noted. Almost like someone who worked with them for a living.

"The next morning it was all over the papers. Heiress killed in car crash. And rumors that she had been murdered by terrorists. I never discovered how they found us, but in some ways I was lucky that everyone else was killed. There was nothing to link me with the business at all. I went underground for a couple of years, and eventually was picked up and made peace, in my way, with the powers. It was all over by then; nothing anyone could do.

"And that, I thought, was the end of it. I was lucky to be alive, and lucky not to be connected with it in any way. When I heard from the magistrate, Balesto, that he was investigating the whole business and wanted to talk to me, I was terrified. I thought, Christ, my luck's run out. I would have made a run for it, but as I was still in jail I couldn't.

"It was Maurizio, of course, who'd put him on to me. He only guessed I had been involved, he had no proof; nobody could do anything much. The magistrate made that clear when he saw me. And he wasn't interested in me anyway. In effect, he offered me immunity from prosecution for anything that might turn up in the future in return for a full statement. So I gave it."

"You trusted him? Might I ask why? It hardly fits in with everything else I know about you, at least then."

"No. You're right. In theory I had no confidence that he'd keep his word. It was something even more disreputable and infantile." She stopped and smiled quietly. "I felt guilty. I'd liked Maria. I needed to make some effort to redress the balance. Even if I wasn't prepared to take many risks and even if I didn't think it would make any difference. I was expecting my first kid by then. Maybe that made the difference. You'll see for yourself, maybe."

Flavia sniffed.

"In some ways, meeting Balesto changed my life, in a small way. He was a good man. Brave in his soul. Do you know what I mean?"

"I think so."

"Unlike me, he believed in justice, and was determined to live up to it, however foolish it was. He took great risks, and they destroyed him for it. Even seeing me was brave; several magistrates had been killed already, and he knew, I think, that he would win no friends in high places by what he was doing.

"He was a very unheroic figure. Short and fat, but he had a sense of himself. A clarity about what he was doing. He was an honest man. I'd never met one before. Have you?"

Flavia nodded. "Maybe one. I used to work for him. As you say, they are rare creatures."

"Anyway, I told him everything, and he nodded and said that he knew most of it already."

"How?"

"He didn't say. Just that it was in his report. Which was almost finished. A week or so later, he was arrested, disgraced, and his papers confiscated."

"So you can't prove any of this."

"Yes. I can. That's the whole point. After Balesto died, Maurizio got a package from him, and in it was a letter, posted by Balesto's lawyer. The letter said that he had done nothing since his arrest, as he was frightened for his family should he speak out. There had been clear threats, which he knew were serious. All his papers had been confiscated when he was arrested, but he had taken the precaution of making and hiding a copy of his investigation and the proof he would need."

"What proof?"

"I don't know. The letter finished by saying that he didn't dare do anything with it himself but, since he knew he was about to die, there was nothing now to lose. If Maurizio wanted the report, he could have it."

"What did it say?"

"I didn't see it. All I saw was the letter; Maurizio came and showed it to me."

"Why?"

"Just to prepare me. He said he was going to have his revenge and he wanted me to have some sleepless nights."

"All this was just to punish you?" Flavia asked incredulously.

"To punish everybody. I was just a minor detail. Anyway, then he vanished. I tried to contact him, but he never answered the phone or returned calls. He just went to earth, and the next I heard was that he was dead. I don't even know if he managed to get the proof."

"It didn't come with the report from the lawyer?"

"No. Balesto said he'd left it long ago with a man called Bottando, who was the one person in the world he knew he could trust to look after it. What's the matter? Have you heard of him?"

Flavia nodded. There wasn't much point in being surprised at anything anymore. "He's my boss. Was, anyway. Go on. What do you mean? That you were just a minor detail?"

Elena looked scornful. "Don't you realize? Don't you know what this is about?"

"It seems not."

"You don't realize that the man who ordered Maria shot was Antonio Sabauda? The man who is now the prime minister? That what Maurizio was going to do was bring down the government?"

Flavia sucked in her breath and stared at her. She had not, in fact, realized that this was what Elena was leading up to. "But you don't know that. You didn't see the report," she protested. She was willing to believe many things of politicians. This was going too far.

"Oh, come on," Elena said angrily. "Sabauda got his big break being tough on terrorists and for his handling of the Di Lanna kidnapping case. He blamed the weak laws, the refusal of parliament to give him stronger powers, and he got everything he wanted. He got the patronage of the Di Lanna family in gratitude for his efforts, and that saw him through all the crises of the next couple of decades. He was also in charge of the security services at the time. Maria's death and the quiet, forceful way Sabauda handled it made his career. He was waiting for something like that to happen, and when it didn't, he made it happen. Dammit, she was taken away by the security services. And the next day she was found dead. Who else do you think killed her?"

"Is that what Maurizio thought?"

"Oh yes. And so did I. When I came out of prison, after Balesto was disgraced, I was visited by the security services. And was told that they had read his report, and knew full well of my role in the Di Lanna case. That I should consider myself lucky to be alive, but that I wouldn't be if ever I told anyone about it."

"So why didn't they kill you? If everybody is as ruthless and murderous as you seem to think?"

She shrugged. "Because you never know when my testimony would come in useful. Sabauda was the friend of the security services, but what if times changed? What if they wanted to bring him down? Then I'd be useful."

"You never thought of leaving the country?"

"Of course. But why bother? They'd find me. But now I am going. That report is out there somewhere, and the security services evidently know it. It's time to pack my bags."

Flavia shook her head. "So what about this picture that Maurizio stole? What was that all about?"

"If this Bottando is your boss, then I think it's fairly obvious. Maurizio wanted a bargaining chip to get this proof. Something to make Bottando give the proof up. Threatening to burn the picture would have been what he had in mind. The report wasn't enough, however damning it might have been."

She shook her head. "No," she said. "That doesn't make sense. If he was going to hand the picture back in exchange for the proof, then what about this business he was planning for Friday?"

Elena shrugged. "There I can't help. As I say, I couldn't get hold of him. I'm only guessing. You're on your own now. And so am I. Don't bother trying to find me. You won't."

18

Argyll may have disliked mobile phones sufficiently to avoid having one himself, but he had fewer scruples about making other people use them. Before he left the cooing turtledoves in their rustic retreat and went back into the village, he borrowed Mary Verney's phone and telephoned Flavia. She, by this time, was also in a bar and also in as much of a reverie as her new teetotal state permitted.

As Argyll knew little of her current paranoid frame of mind, her reluctance to say where she was made him a little irritable. But eventually it dawned on him that, when she said she would meet him in the truffle place, she meant a small restaurant halfway between Florence and Siena where they had spent a blissful few hours a couple of years previously. Why she couldn't have just said so he wasn't entirely certain, nor did he understand why she couldn't have chosen somewhere a little bit closer, but he was, by and large, used to her little ways and drove there as quickly as possible. She said she had important news. He said the same. Each doubted that the other's news could possibly be more important than his or her own.

In the end, when they'd met, begged a table even though the restaurant was closed, and talked for a good hour, Argyll reckoned Flavia was ahead by a length. Being pregnant, watched by the security services, and on the track of evidence that the prime minister of Italy was a murderer were marginally more surprising items, in his opinion, than discovering the lovers' tryst at Mary Verney's Tuscan hideaway, especially as he omitted some of his imaginary extrapolations. At least Argyll could answer one of her questions. Why Bottando?

"When Bottando was in Florence, back in the sixties, this magistrate took a shine to him. Thought he was very able. Wrote letters of commendation. It was in the police report at Buonaterra I told you about. It probably helped his career quite a lot. Bottando owed him. Shall we go and ask?"

"I suppose." She looked out of the window and smiled. "If these people would leave me alone, I think I'd happily forget the whole thing. Do you know, at the moment, I couldn't give two hoots about the prime minister, or long past murders, or whether Claudes disappear or not? Do you know what I want to do?"

"No."

"I want to paint the apartment. I've been thinking about it all day."

"What?"

"Hmm. Odd, isn't it?"

"Extremely. Wouldn't it be better to sort out one or two other things first? Like being able to get back into the apartment safely?"

"Maybe. But I've been working for years without a serious break, and I want to do nothing but water the plants. The shopping. And what I am doing instead is fighting off an attempt to oust me from my job so that I won't be able to do any of these things."

"So why bother? Why not quit?"

"Are you serious?"

"Of course I am."

"What would I do? I mean, bringing up baby is one thing, but I wouldn't want to spend my life doing it. Besides, even generous payoffs don't last forever. Then what?"

Argyll considered. The idea of Flavia applying her considerable energies and intelligence to nothing more demanding than finding the most absorbent diapers did frighten him somewhat. "We could set up together. Finding pictures. You know. The stuff you never heard of because people avoid the police. We could have Bottando as a consultant . . ."

"And Mary Verney?" she added, a touch sarcastically.

"You must admit she'd be an asset. And charge clients a fortune for a discreet and effective service."

"Assuming we could find the clients and provide the service."

"Would that be so difficult?"

"Yes. You don't just run around asking questions and producing pictures out of a hat, you know. Without files, background material, colleagues, you'd never get anywhere."

"None of those have been much use in this case."

"This case is an oddity. And don't think that I or Bottando could play on our contacts for long to get official information. The moment you're out, that's it. All I—or Bottando—would be able to get would be crumbs."

"Just an idea. I was briefly entertaining notions of moving, you see."

"What do you mean? Why should we move?"

"Babies. Diapers. Do you have any idea how much space these things take up? Our apartment is scarcely big enough for us as it is without trying to add truckloads of brightly colored plastic toys and things."

"We can't afford a bigger one."

"Not if we stay in Rome," he said thoughtfully.

"You wouldn't want to leave Rome, would you? Not seriously?" She couldn't have been more astonished if he'd suggested joining the army.

He looked at her sadly. "I don't know," he said mournfully. "Just feeling itchy, I suppose."

"Shall we go?" she prompted, when she decided the dreamy look had been on his face quite long enough.

"Where?"

"To go and ask Bottando about all this."

"Eh? Oh, that. Yes. I suppose."

"You haven't said anything about my news."

"No. I'm still in shock."

"Are you pleased? Or not?"

"I'm pleased," he said carefully, then threw caution to the winds. "I'm delighted," he added. "Absolutely delighted. I'm so pleased that . . ."

"All right, all right," she said quickly. She wasn't used to him getting emotional and it made her feel slightly uncomfortable. "Don't get carried away. I was just checking. Come on."

So back they went again. A quiet journey. Flavia was half asleep, and Argyll was busy thinking about the implications of what Flavia called her news. He would, no doubt, get the hang of it eventually, but it was a bit of a shock.

Sensible people would, no doubt, have gone straight to sleep the moment they arrived and begun business the next morning, but only Flavia felt tired and she was determined to stay awake as long as possible. So Mary Verney lit the lamps on the terrace, got out the bottles of water for Flavia and the grappa for everyone else, and they all sat around in the quiet night air, talking softly.

Flavia began, listing her trials, tribulations, and her news. For some reason, the news took pride of place; the trials and tribulations seemed minor in comparison. Then she got down to the serious business.

And it was all so terribly simple. Once she'd finished, Bottando smiled.

"Well done." I should have guessed you'd figure it all out. Stupid of me not to tell you beforehand, really."

"Why didn't you? I find it all a little hurtful."

"I didn't for the same reason most people being blackmailed keep quiet. Sabbatini made it clear that if there was any outside involvement he'd burn the picture. I read the file on him, and decided he was quite loopy enough to do it. So I thought I'd play safe until I got it back."

"So? What happened?"

"About twenty minutes after you came to tell me about your meeting with the prime minister, I got a phone call from Sabbatini. Saying he wanted this piece of paper the magistrate Balesto had given me, and would swap the picture for it. No deals, negotiations, concessions. Simple as that. Or else.

"I was astonished. I hadn't even thought about it for nearly twenty years. After all, this investigation of Balesto's was more or less unofficial; he never told me he was working on it. All I knew was that he asked me to look after an envelope for him. He was an old friend by then. He'd been good to me when I was young and we kept up contact; I went to see him every time I went to Florence, and he came to see me when he came to Rome. It was only about once a year, sometimes even less.

"When he handed it over, he didn't tell me what was in it, nor did I ask. I just put it in a file, and forgot about it. And if that sounds strange, it wasn't; he was a friend, and I was happy to do him a service without any quibbles or curiosity. It could have been anything, a copy of his will, for all I knew.

"I never saw him again, although I tried to. When he was bounced out of the magistracy I wrote to him expressing my sympathies, and saying that I didn't believe a word of the complaints against him, but got no reply. I even went to his house once, but was turned away. He went into private practice and spent the rest of his life defending petty criminals and speeding drivers. He saw no one, dropped all his friends, including me. I was very hurt by it, but eventually I gave up. If he didn't want to see me, there was not much I could do about it."

"His letter to Sabbatini suggested his family had been threatened."

"Really? Maybe so. Perhaps he wasn't prepared even to risk
being seen with me. Whatever, I forgot about his envelope and
would never have remembered it if that idiot Sabbatini hadn't
started threatening me. In the circumstances, I couldn't really do
much except agree to what he wanted. I opened the envelope, of
course; but it meant nothing to me. It was a bank statement."

"Whose?"

"I have no idea. An anonymous account in Belgium, detailing
payments to another in Milan. Just numbers, no names. Quite a
lot of money, especially for 1981. Five payments of twenty-five
thousand dollars, between June and September. As I say, it meant
nothing to me, and I didn't know why Sabbatini wanted it. But if
that was the price of a Claude, so be it. I photocopied it and went
to the agreed meeting place on a country lane about twenty miles
south of Rome. I was to stop in a lay-by and wait outside the car,
and he would come along later.

"Sabbatini, of course, tried to be clever about it. He arrived in a
white van, stopped, and opened the door to let me see the picture
inside. I showed him the bank statement, and the look of triumph
on his face suggested it was just what he was expecting and what he
wanted. When I asked what it was all about, he pulled a gun on me,
and said I would find out on Friday. Then he drove off with the envelope, the picture, and the keys to my car."

Flavia nodded. "Fine, if embarrassing. But . . ."

"I was a little annoyed, as you can imagine," Bottando went on
gravely. "Not least because I was faced with the possibility of having
to come to you and confess how stupid I'd been. So before I did, I
thought I'd see if I could repair the damage. I hardly expected to
find him in his flat or his studio, of course, but thoroughness and a
lack of anywhere else to look meant I had to start there. When I got
to his apartment, the lights were on, so I waited outside for nearly

four hours. And in the end, it wasn't Sabbatini at all who came out, but a short fat little man carrying a bundle under his arm who got into a black Alfa Romeo and was driven off. The dark hand of the state, I thought, so I decided that things were probably back under control. My panic subsided a little and I went to his studio.

"Not there either. I knew he was supposedly doing an exhibition so I went as a last resort to the gallery where he was showing, or performing, or whatever he called it. Back door was open, and there he was in the vat of plaster, which wasn't set. He was perfectly dead. Now, if you think about it, is it likely that someone who had just pulled off a stunt like that would go back and start rehearsing some damn fool art thing? My suspicion was that the people in the apartment and his presence in the tub were connected, and that he'd been pushed under and held there until he drowned.

"I talked it over with Mary—I would have talked it over with you by that stage, my dear, but I thought that the less you knew the better—and decided that it might be best to keep well out of it. I wasn't joking when I said I wanted nothing to jeopardize my retirement, and this was nasty. Then the whole business of the ransom demand began. I didn't understand it—still don't, in fact—but at least it was simple. I was merely concerned that you should not be there at the handover. It was potentially very dangerous indeed, so I bullied you into staying in the car. If anyone was going to get shot because I was stupid, then it really would better be me. The rest was as you imagine, except that the person who collected the money didn't really resemble Sabbatini. But don't ask me what he did look like, as I didn't see him very well."

Flavia digested all of this, although what was at the forefront of her mind really was the desire for a whiskey and a cigarette. "Not your finest hour," she said dryly after a while.

Bottando looked suitably mortified.

"Elena Fortini thinks that Maria di Lanna was murdered on the orders of Sabauda, and that Maurizio was going after him."

"And was going to get the news irretrievably into the public domain by burning the painting?" Bottando said. "Possible. I think he was right that he would have needed something quite dramatic to avoid the story being hushed up. No good just going to the papers, they wouldn't have touched it."

"It still doesn't answer why that particular picture," she said grumpily.

"Does it matter?"

"No. Just a detail. But he went to a lot of trouble and if all he wanted was something that would catch the attention there were simpler ways of going about it."

"I thought you reckoned it had some cunning meaning," Argyll said.

"Evidently not. I can't see any connection. The painting's story has got a happy ending."

"No, it hasn't."

"Yes, it has. Macchioli told me."

"That's the sanitized Renaissance version where everything has to come right. I looked it up for you. In the real thing, poor old Procris gets popped with Cephalus's magic arrow and that's it. No goddess to bring her back."

"So?"

"So nothing. I just thought I'd demonstrate my superior powers of research. You always did say that Sabbatini was a bit weak on ideas."

Bottando would have become impatient with the way the conversation was going had not the warm night air and soft light on the terrace lulled him and everyone else into a surprisingly peaceful mood. Four people who knew each other well, enjoying a relaxing evening together, talking, speaking softly in the way you do when the light fades to streaks of pinkish blue and the only sounds come from the cicadas in the woods.

"As for Sabauda, I don't know. It's always been known that the security services were every bit as violent as the terrorists. Saying they acted on direct orders is a big leap, though. And I can't see how that bank statement helps. Unless the report explained it. But as we don't have the report, and only have a photocopy of the statement . . ."

He paused, distracted by a noise that seemed to be getting louder. An intrusive bumping and scraping of metal suggested that someone was driving, badly, down the stony, irregular path that led to the house. He looked at Mary, who shrugged. Not expecting anyone.

A few seconds later, an ancient red Fiat chugged into view and pulled up outside, its little engine heaving with effort. The driver switched off the engine, making the sudden silence seem all the more remarkable, and then got out, slamming the door in irritation.

"Oh, God, it's Dossoni," Flavia said, peering at the figure, dimly lit by the terrace lights. It was the night air, she thought afterward. That was why she felt nothing more than mild irritation. An unwelcome guest, breaking the atmosphere. Not one of the party. An interloper into their conversation.

"Who?"

"The journalist and police informer," she said, as the sweating reporter walked around to peer in the faint light at the wing of the car, dented badly when he drove into a boulder halfway up the track. He seemed from his movements to be very cross. "Don't know which is worse."

Dossoni kicked the car, then turned to the house and walked purposefully toward them. "You should do something about that driveway," he called angrily from a distance of about thirty meters.

"It's a track, not a driveway," Mary Verney said mildly. "What do you think this is, the suburbs of Milan?"

Dossoni snorted. "Well, at least it still goes."

"Good evening," Flavia said. "What are you doing here? How did you find us?"

"Oh, easy enough. Tapped your mobile phone. Traced the call your husband made to you. One of these little devices. You can buy them in shops these days. Amazing little things."

"I see. But what do you want?"

"Well, two things. First, I was wondering if you knew where to find Elena Fortini."

"I thought you wouldn't go near her," Flavia said, noticing the permanent sheen of sweat on Dossoni's forehead shining in the lamplight, giving him a slightly unearthly appearance.

"I've changed my mind."

"I don't know. She was planning to disappear. It seems she probably has."

"Damnation."

"Might I ask what you want her for?"

Dossoni looked slightly embarrassed as he pulled out a gun from his pocket. He looked at it quizzically, as though he was wondering how it had got there. "I was sort of planning to kill her," he said, his voice dropping to a whisper as if he too was reluctant to disturb the calm. "Just as I think I shall have to kill all four of you. I'm sorry about that."

He pointed the gun at Flavia.

"Just a second." Mary Verney spoke in the fluttering tone of voice that Argyll recognized as the one she used when she was about to do something unfortunate. "Why, exactly, are you going to kill us? It's a bit rude, you know."

Dossoni considered whether to reply, then evidently decided it made no real difference. "I want to ensure that certain matters do not become generally known. Which means getting hold of certain documents that should remain confidential, and ensuring that those people who know of their existence remain silent. Does that make you feel better?"

He smiled apologetically.

"Oh, dear," Mary Verney said, wringing her hands. "I'm afraid you make no sense to me at all. But I assure you, young man, that killing us won't be necessary. Will it, Jonathan?"

"I don't think so," Argyll said, after considering the question objectively.

"Well, I do think so," Dossoni replied, still quiet. Maybe it was the darkness, maybe the gun that now made him so calm. "I don't want something accusing me of murdering that woman getting into the wrong hands."

"We don't have anything," Flavia said.

"I know that," Dossoni said, almost apologetically. "I got everything from Sabbatini. But you know about it, you see. So . . ."

Flavia looked at him. "Did you kill her? That poor woman?"

"Yes."

"Why?"

"Because I was told to. And I do what I am told. Just as I did with Sabbatini. Now I think it's time to work on my own for once."

"Who told you?"

He shook his head. "Sorry."

"I don't suppose we might persuade you to go away?" Mary asked.

"I doubt it."

"Look," she said, her voice suddenly hysterical. She picked up a brown briefcase, making Dossoni swing his gun around to her. "Please don't do this. You'd regret it later, I know you would. There's some money in here, you know. The general went to the bank this morning. You can have it all. All his pension money for the next two months . . ."

Dossoni looked wearied by all this nonsense, checked his gun meticulously, and walked behind Argyll's chair. He put the gun to Argyll's head.

To say that Argyll was frightened would be to understate the matter. He closed his eyes, and tried to keep the panic under control. He looked at Mary Verney, and was strangely reassured. It was her eyes, measuring, watching, and assessing. As she twittered and fluttered—oh, watch out, that might be loaded—she seemed to know exactly what she was doing. Unfortunately, Argyll didn't, which was why he was not completely relaxed.

"Be quiet," Dossoni said.

"Do be careful, young man," Mary went on, babbling as aging ladies who have never experienced danger before are prone to do. "Accidents will happen, you know. I remember when my cousin Charles was cleaning his Purdey. Back in 1953, this was. No, I tell a lie, it must have been 1954 . . ."

"Shut up, you stupid old woman," Dossoni snapped. But he pulled the gun away from Argyll and pointed it at her to emphasize the importance of silence. Mary Verney let out a short scream of fright, and dropped the briefcase. She flustered and fluttered on the ground to pick it all up again, twittering about losing all the general's papers. "He's a very important man, you know . . ."

Dossoni evidently had had enough. He took two steps toward her but, before he could do much more, Mary Verney looked up, took aim very methodically, and shot him three times in the chest with the gun she had taken from Bottando's briefcase.

The noise was appalling. So was the effect. The impact of the bullets lifted Dossoni off the ground and hurled him backward onto Argyll, who squealed in terror and tried to wriggle out from underneath. The smell was terrible, the sight worse. When Argyll did get free, he scuttled behind the table before peering out. The cicadas were still twittering, the light from the lamps around the terrace still reflected peacefully off the glasses of red wine and made the thick gathering pools of blood shine in a way that, Argyll thought quite irrelevantly, reminded him of a painting he had once seen. The execution of St. Catherine on the wheel. Venetian. Very much into strong, bold coloration, the Venetians. Giorgione? Maybe not. He couldn't remember, and then he remembered it really wasn't that important at the moment.

Neither Bottando nor Flavia had moved. They just sat there, watching and saying nothing. There was little enough to say, after all. Things like "goodness," or "dear me" were inadequate for the occasion, and shouting or screaming seemed a little pointless.

Apart from the body slumped over Argyll's chair, the pools of blood all over the floor, the smell and the sight of Mary Verney sitting with the gun in her hand, coolly looking, everything was perfectly normal.

"What have you done?" Argyll managed to say eventually, after he'd watched her go over, feel the man's pulse, and rummage in his pockets. "Where did you get that gun from?"

"This?" she asked. "Oh, it's Taddeo's. He forgot to hand it in when he retired. Very careless of him to keep it loaded. Although, in the circumstances, I think we might forgive him this time. Grappa, I think."

She was remarkably calm. Frighteningly so. She poured the drinks with a steady hand, while Argyll could scarcely hold his glass, his were trembling so much. It was why, he thought, she made such a good thief and he would have been such a terrible one. He found her more terrifying than Dossoni.

"He was going to kill us, you know," she said reassuringly. "Don't think he was just saying that for fun. Or that we might have talked him out of it. Just a question of whether you want him dead, or us."

"Did you have to kill him, though?"

"What did you expect me to do? Shoot the gun out of his hands? My eyesight's so bad I was lucky to hit him at all. I don't get a great deal of practice in this sort of thing, you know."

"But what do we do now?" Maybe it was something about the shock that made him prone to asking fatuous questions.

She thought. "We have two choices. We either get rid of the body . . ."

"Or what?" It was getting worse.

"Or we call the police."

"What about if he has friends down the road?"

"Then we're in trouble. I was assuming he was on his own. In fact, he must have been. This has all the signs of a do-it-yourself affair. Hurried, badly planned. This is not the way you go about killing people if you're professional about it."

Argyll shook his head. It was a bit too bizarre for him. There she was, sixty if she was a day, gray hair done up in a bun, gun in hand, talking as though assassinating people was as common as baking a fruit cake.

"I think under the circumstances that calling the police might be unwise just at the moment," Bottando said quietly, finally shaking off his shock. "It would be best if one or two things were settled first."

"Such as?" Argyll said crossly. Was he the only person here going to show any sign of alarm or upset at what had happened? Was he really the only one who regarded a bloodstained body on the terrace as a little out of the ordinary?

"I think we have to make sure there is no repetition," he said. "Flavia?"

She nodded, and got up in a dreamy fashion. "Yes," she said. "Shall we go?"

"Where?"

"To Rome. To sort things out," she said. "We're going to talk to Di Lanna. He's the only one with enough power to do anything. We will have to get his protection, in effect. I only hope he'll give it. But if we give him his wife's murderer he should owe us something. It's just a pity we can't give him any proof."

"Just a moment," Argyll said petulantly. "What about this?" He waved his hand in the direction of the body. "You can't just leave him there."

Bottando looked thoughtful. "No. You'll have to move it."

"*Me?* Why should *I* move it?"

"You can't expect Mary to. She's not strong enough. And you shouldn't sound so annoyed. If it wasn't for Mary you'd be dead."

"And now," said Mary Verney, as they watched the lights of Bottando's car disappear down the track as he and Flavia headed for Rome. "Perhaps you'd be so kind as to remove that corpse from my terrace, Jonathan?"

Argyll, who thought her levity was a little distasteful, scowled at her. "No," he said. He was beginning to resent being the only normal person left in the world.

"Oh, but you must. You heard the general. I can hardly do it myself, and what if the police should come? Or the grocer? What would they say?"

"I don't care. I'm not going to move him until you are honest with me. I know it doesn't come naturally. It will be an effort, but you'll have to try. Otherwise you'll be stuck with Signor Dossoni on your terrace for the next week."

"Very threatening of you. And quite insulting, too. I always try to be honest. Most of the time. What do you want to know, exactly?"

"The money. Where is it?"

"What money?"

"The three million dollars."

"Oh. That money."

"That money."

She looked at him, hesitated, then let out a deep breath. "It's in Switzerland. I took it there last Monday. It's in a bank."

"In your name?"

"Well, yes. Since you ask. It is."

Here she stopped, so Argyll prompted her. "And how did you get hold of it?"

"If you must be so nosy," she said, "it's simple enough. Taddeo told me what he was going to do, and I was worried. So I tagged along in my little car and saw the whole encounter, from Sabbatini arriving to his driving off in his van with the picture still inside it. And saw Taddeo hopping up and down in the lay-by looking furious. I followed, at a discreet distance, until Sabbatini stopped at a petrol station. Have you ever noticed that when the excitement fades all you are left with is a profound need to go to the toilet?"

Argyll said that his life was blessedly free of excitement, most of the time. Although now she mentioned it . . .

He disappeared into the house for a few moments, and then came back. "You were saying?" he said, as Mary showed no signs of volunteering information without constant prodding.

"Well, that's how it was with Sabbatini. He ran for the toilet as fast as his legs would carry him, and while he was there, I stole his van."

She smiled. Argyll scowled. "Just like that," he said.

"Pretty much. I mean, he'd taken the keys out, but it was an old van and that was no great trouble. So there we are. Simple, really."

"And then you hoodwinked the general into thinking . . ."

"Good heavens, no."

Argyll looked at her for a few moments as it all sank in. "No?" he said. "You mean that he knew all about this? He decided to take the money? After all this time he's become a criminal?"

Mary Verney looked puzzled. "Don't be silly," she said. "It's a great embarrassment to both of us. Who wants three million dollars? Do you have any idea how difficult it is to manage that amount of dirty money?"

Argyll said he hadn't.

"It's no easy business. I have quite enough, thank you very much, and Taddeo's tastes are terribly modest when he's not in a restaurant. No. We kept the money as we didn't know what else to do. Sabbatini had been killed, the secret services had gone through his apartment. Taddeo knew the murder had to be something to do with the Di Lanna business and simply did not want to get involved.

Can you blame him, considering what's been going on here? If he'd suddenly turned up with the picture, then he would have had to explain how he got it. Much better to convince everyone that the plot was all to do with money by inventing some nonexistent collaborator for Sabbatini and by keeping it all as distant as possible. At least, that seemed the best idea at the time."

"You could have told Flavia."

"She would have been obliged to do something. He did his best to keep her out of it and tried to get her to leave well enough alone. If she'd done as she was told and forgotten about it—as the general told her to, the prime minister told her to, Di Lanna told her to and, I imagine, you told her to as well—then all would have been well. As it is, we now have a mess on our hands."

"You can't blame her for all this."

"I'm not blaming anyone. All I know is, if Taddeo had just turned up and handed in the picture, people would have asked how he got it."

"You could have found it in a ditch."

"Don't be silly. We couldn't get away with that approach twice. Nearly didn't the first time. Now. Will you *please* clean up this mess?"

"Just a second," Argyll said sternly. "I didn't mean last week. I meant now. You could have told her now that you had the money. Why didn't you?" He scrutinized her face very closely. "You're going to keep it, aren't you," he said accusingly.

At least she had the grace to look a little embarrassed.

"After forty years of impeccable, legendary honesty, Bottando comes across you again and within weeks he's walking off with three million dollars stuffed down his trouser leg." He shook his head. "You really are quite something."

"We can worry about all that later," she said, pointing once more to Dossoni.

"Let's worry about it now."

"Why?"

"Because you have more money than you need, so you say, and, thanks to you two geriatric hooligans, Flavia is out of a job. And because if you didn't have dishonorable notions about hanging on to the stuff, you would have had no trouble telling Flavia all about it. But you didn't. Bottando told her a direct lie and said he'd handed over the money. A lie, which speaks volumes."

She grimaced in the manner of someone about to explain something very simple to someone even simpler.

"Jonathan, what were we meant to do with the money? It would have been such a waste to give it back. After all, it was the price of getting the picture back and the picture was returned. I recovered it. And I don't work for nothing, you know."

"And Bottando agreed?"

"After I'd worked on him a bit. It's remarkable the effect being eased out of a job has on even the most upright of people."

"Well, I'm not going to be the one to tell all this to Flavia."

"I should hope not. She'd be most upset. She quite possibly wouldn't understand."

"But silence, as they say, is an expensive commodity. So we might be able to help each other."

Mary Verney looked closely at him. "Dear me," she said. "So much for the quiet and inoffensive scholar routine."

"It's the company I keep," he replied. "It rubs off on you. Besides, we putative fathers have to go a-hunting and a-gathering, you know."

"Very well," she said with a sigh. "It's a deal. We can sort the details out later, no doubt. Or do you distrust me that much?"

"I would never dream of it. Now, this corpse . . ."

They walked tentatively back to look at Dossoni's body lying on the ground. Then Mary got a thick tarpaulin from the house, they wrapped him in it with great distaste, and dragged him slowly to his car.

"I suppose we'd better put him in the boot," he said calmly. It was amazing what you could get used to. "That's what you people normally do, isn't it?"

"What do you mean, 'you people'? I don't make a habit of this, you know."

"You'd never know." He opened the trunk and peered inside with a torch. There was a jumble of tools, and bits of paper, and old sandwich wrappers and newspapers. Argyll cleared them all to one side to make room. Then he saw the thick brown envelope.

He looked at it, and thought, then picked it up and peered inside. And realization dawned. With his hands trembling, he shook out the contents of the big envelope. He opened the cover and read "Report on the murder of Signora Maria di Lanna on May . . ."

"Oh, my God," he said. "He had it in his car all the time. He hadn't handed it in. He was going to keep it for himself."

The body quite forgotten, propped up against the side of the car as though he was having a nap, Mary Verney and Argyll sat down to read in the light of the Fiat's headlights. And as they read, Argyll's blood began to run cold, and panic came over him once more, but far more violently.

"Dear God. She's walking into a death trap," he said quietly, after they'd scanned the summary at the end.

He ran back into the house, picked up the phone, and dialed her mobile. Within seconds, a chirruping began to come from the handbag Flavia had left behind her by the table on the terrace. He stared at it aghast.

"Take your car. Drive to Rome. Find them both. If you're lucky you'll be in time."

Argyll looked at her. "But . . ."

"I'll take care of this one. Don't worry. There's a nice forest about fifty kilometers from here. Then I'll hose down the terrace. Go, Jonathan. Hurry."

19

The closer they got to Rome, the more nervous Flavia became, so nervous that even her unaccustomed car sickness began to fade. The shock of seeing Dossoni shot finally began to affect her; she felt cold, shivery, and numb. She constantly looked around to see if they were being followed, scrutinizing every policeman to see if there was any flicker of recognition when the man saw Bottando's car or her face. Even worse, her mood communicated itself to Bottando, so much so that he took a detour to cruise past the entrance to Flavia's apartment, slowing down just enough to see the black Fiat still parked down the street, two men strategically posted front and back. Bottando grunted; there was no need for further comment.

Then they went on to Bottando's apartment. Again, the car. Again the watchful pair of eyes.

"Damnation," Flavia said. "They'll have searched it."

"Just as well I didn't tidy it up before I left, then," Bottando said perfectly calmly.

He had stopped the car while they looked, then pulled out, turned sharp right, and drove away as discreetly as possible.

"I think they saw you."

"I know they did," he replied. "But I bet I know this part of town better than they do. Never overestimate the intelligence of these people."

There was no proof that he was right, but no proof either that he was overly optimistic; Flavia saw no sign of any following car. Bottando drove them to a residential district behind the Vatican, where they sat waiting for the day to begin. They didn't talk; Bottando seemed preoccupied and once turned to Flavia to tell her something, but she had fallen asleep and was breathing softly and peacefully. He looked at her with affection mixed with regret, then let her be. He could not sleep himself.

When the first bars and cafés finally began to open he woke her up, and they went to have coffee and something to eat. Flavia washed as best she could to wake herself up, then Bottando drove to the Colosseum and parked on a side street. They walked to the Metro station—in one end, out the other—then onto the first passing bus. They got off at the Capitoline, then became tourists, walking into the Forum just as it opened. They strolled among the ruins, finally finding a secluded jumble of rubble where they could sit and talk. All around the early tourists walked, snapping with their cameras, consulting their guidebooks, looking with frowns on their faces from plans to reality then back again, trying to make sense of what they saw.

"We don't have a very strong hand here, do we? We don't have either the report or the proof. Presumably Dossoni got both of them. All we have is a photocopy, which isn't much use. There's nothing much we can do."

Bottando nodded. "True. And against us we seem to have at least bits of the secret service, and a desperate prime minister. There's nothing we can do about that; no chance of righting wrongs or seeing justice is done, I think. All we can do is try and immunize ourselves. Di Lanna's the only person who might help us." He heaved a heavy sigh. "You can always offer him his money back," he said gloomily. "That might help."

She looked at him. "We don't have it," she pointed out.

"Well . . ." he began.

"It doesn't matter anyway," she interrupted. "Even if we did have it, I'm damned if I see why I should offer anybody anything back."

"Pardon?"

"No. Enough's enough. If we can get hold of the money, we keep it. We might well need it more than Di Lanna ever will. We're faced with the prospect of being pursued without end. Especially now Dossoni is dead. I hate to say it, but if this doesn't work and Di Lanna won't help we'll probably have to go into hiding, at least for a bit. I don't want to stay around to see how much the prime minister wants to remain in office."

"You're beginning to sound like Mary."

"Sensible women looking after idealistic men. Don't tell Jonathan. He'd be appalled." She shook her head in disbelief. "A week ago I was head of the art theft squad, you know," she said. "Now I'm sitting on a stone talking about going on the run with a suitcase full of dodgy money. What happened?"

"Prime ministers," Bottando said. "You can't say I didn't warn you."

They sat there for another half hour or more, considering other options, such as going to a magistrate or the newspapers—with what? Bottando asked—but came up with nothing. So it was decided. They stood up and looked at each other.

"Good luck," Bottando said quietly. "You're going to need it. You sure you don't want me to come?"

She shook her head. "No. I know him. We got on quite well. Best me alone." She smiled wanly. "All I want to do is paint the kitchen, you know."

He smiled. "And all I want to do is enjoy a long and quiet retirement. I'm sorry I got you into this mess."

"I'm sorry I got myself into it. You always did say prime ministers can ruin your life. I didn't think you meant it quite so literally."

Then she gave him a quick peck on the cheek and walked away.

From then on, Flavia's biggest problem was her nerves. She was convinced that, at any moment, someone would leap out from behind a lamppost and shoot her.

In fact, nothing of the sort happened. She bought herself a hat from a stand selling trinkets to tourists to hide her face, then walked to the Chamber of Deputies. No one paid her any attention. She attached herself to a group of tourists and strolled into the building without having to show any identification. Shocking lapse of security. And she walked along the dingy corridors to Di Lanna's office without anyone asking her business, or looking at her strangely. But just as she was about to reach the relative safety of his office, she hesitated, and walked on until she came to a little bench and sat down.

She was breathing deeply, almost panting, as she struggled to get a grip on her reluctance. It was something Argyll had said. What was it? Something about one artist's style hiding another. What was that about? That little examination Bulovius had subjected him to. So what? Why did that stick in her mind? And why was it joined to his description of the Claude? Not a happy ending after all, that's what he'd said.

She thought back and back to her school days. Classical mythology. They'd had to do it when they were about twelve. The more she thought, the more it receded toward the horizon. She sat there for five minutes, maybe longer, her brain refusing to hand over the memories she needed. Why had Sabbatini gone after that particular picture? This was the question she'd asked again and again. Why was he so precise? Eventually, she shook her head and got up. There was no point in delaying any further.

This time there was a secretary guarding the entrance. She told her that she wasn't expected, but that the deputy would see her. It was an urgent matter.

A few minutes later, he did. She went into the poky inner office, and Di Lanna rose from his chair to welcome her, waving her to the same wooden seat she had sat in not long before. He smiled; that same, slightly sad, unpolitical smile.

"Good morning, signora. I am glad to see you again. I hope you have some good news for me this time."

Flavia opened her mouth to speak, then stopped as all the comments and all the questions suddenly came together in a great panoramic whole. Her brain was spinning, she felt dizzy from the realization of what it all meant. Of course it was true. Just as Argyll insisted that a flicker of instinct must sometimes overwhelm a vast mass of evidence in attributing a painting, so it was the same with crimes.

And there was suddenly no doubt whatsoever in her mind. Years of experience and training had fine-tuned her sensibilities, made her aware of contradictions and loose ends. She was very good at her job, she realized, and knew at the same moment that her instinct was all for nothing. What a waste, she thought absently, and noticed that she really didn't care very much.

"I don't think so," she said, fighting to get her breath under control. "But I don't suppose you will find it too bad."

"Please continue."

"I imagine you have just had your office swept of all those listening devices, is that correct?"

He nodded.

"In that case we can drop all the pretense and talk plainly. I've come to offer you a deal," she said. "I'd like to have you arrested, but practically speaking I don't think it's possible."

He looked quizzical and amused. "Arrested?" he said mockingly. "Dear me. Whatever for?"

"For the murder of your wife and your brother-in-law," she said quietly. "Not that you killed them yourself, of course. Dossoni did that for you."

His face had gone stony, immobile, and frightening. Had she made a mistake? She had just accused him of the worst possible crime. No one should get away with it. But he had, and he was going to. There was nothing Flavia could do about it. She would have to be very clever just to stay alive herself.

Di Lanna spoke again, all the easygoing, relaxed charm gone from his voice. "This conclusion is based on what reasoning or evidence?"

And now it was time to lie. How could she say she had never seen the report composed by the magistrate, that she was guessing what it said by interpreting Sabbatini's crazy behavior? The symbol of the act; and she was reading and interpreting the symbols, using them to grasp something that was forever beyond her reach.

She could not possibly say that she had reached her conclusions because Sabbatini had so carefully chosen a particular picture by Claude to steal, that when he had read in the papers about the picture's arriving he had gone straight forward, his indecision overcome. Because the true story of Cephalus and Procris doesn't end happily; rather, Cephalus shoots the wife he had so recently married with the arrow she had given him, and no goddess brings her back to life again. Procris gives him power, and he uses it to kill her.

Maria had brought her husband power through her family's money, and Di Lanna had used it to kill her. That was what the bank statements would show: a transfer of funds to Dossoni for carrying out the murder. And after that, Di Lanna used his righteous grief to move against Maria's brother, to have him removed as a beneficiary of the father's trusts. He took most for himself, and became a power in the land. Who could do anything about him? All the politicians were in his debt, everyone knew what had happened to Balesto. Di Lanna was untouchable. If he fell, so did everyone else.

But she didn't say any of this. She guessed, and hoped instead. "This is based on the Balesto report, and on the transcripts of banking transactions that he also discovered."

Di Lanna smiled. "I don't think so," he said.

"Because Dossoni recovered them? True, he did. But he didn't give them to you, did he? He started working for himself."

"What makes you think that?"

"He told me. But you needn't worry about him."

"No? Why is that?"

"He's dead. That's what I came to tell you."

"So you are now the only person who knows anything about this?"

"That's right. What happened?"

He considered for a moment, then shrugged. "The picture disappeared, and I was sent a fax. A photocopy of a page from Ovid. Maurizio being certain that I got the message. Typical of him. It should have been obvious but, as usual, his mind was so tortuous that what he did couldn't be understood without an explanation. So I contacted Dossoni. To clean up. But he seems to have decided to take advantage of the situation. I'd paid him off before, but once he killed Maurizio and got the report he became more demanding. When the ransom demand arrived I knew it came from Dossoni. Three million dollars. I paid it. You understand, no doubt, why I wanted this dropped?"

"Crystal clear."

"How much do you want now?" he asked wearily

"Nothing. You will never find the reports or the proof. And I will never use them unless I am provoked. I will leave you alone and, in return, you will leave me alone."

"Why is that?"

"How long has the prime minister known about this?" she went on, ignoring his question.

"Since the moment it happened. Why do you think I'm his

biggest supporter?" He looked at her sadly. "I've had this hanging over my head for years now."

"What do you want? Sympathy?"

"No. For the last six months, members of my party have been talking about pulling out of the government. This whole business, sending the report to Maurizio, was a warning from Sabauda. If I stepped out of line, he'd destroy me."

"I thought the report was sent to him by the magistrate."

Di Lanna looked scornful. "Don't be ridiculous. This was one of Sabauda's dirty tricks."

"He can't do without you, you daren't do without him."

"That's about it."

"I cannot think of a bigger punishment for either of you, then. You deserve each other. If I could put you behind bars, I would. But I doubt whether I could take on you *and* the government." Di Lanna smiled in agreement.

"But you can't touch me either. Lift a finger, and the report gets published. It might not finish you off, but it would damage you. Embroil you in lawsuits with your trustees for the rest of your life. Bring your career as party leader to an end. That I could do, I think. With the report and the proof."

Which I don't have, she thought.

He nodded. "Yes," he said reasonably, "that you could do. If I lose control of the trusts, then I lose the party. That is true. But you say you are not going to. Why not?"

"Because I am sick of you all. Stick you in jail and you're replaced by someone just as bad. Why bother? All it would do is make my life miserable and in the end you'd survive anyway. You people always do. I want away from all this."

He nodded.

"So, are we agreed?"

He nodded again.

"Good," she went on; "then you are also going to intervene

with the ministry to give me the biggest payoff in the history of the police force. And then we will have a standoff. You leave me alone. I leave you alone. Both of us know the consequences of breaking our word."

She stood up. He did the same, and held out his hand. She ignored it, and walked out.

She left his office and the building, breath coming in short sharp gasps once more, her head swimming with the effects of nausea, running to get through the main entrance of the chamber and into the sunshine beyond. She didn't even remember that Argyll, who ran up to her with an anxious look on his face, having been searching the streets for her for hours, should still have been in Tuscany.

Instead, she threw up on his shoes before he could say anything.

20

If the size of the Flavia's severance package was any indication of Di Lanna's willingness to keep to his side of the bargain, then they were safe indeed. Breaths were sucked in, lips puckered, clouds of envy wafted swiftly over the faces of colleagues like scudding clouds in the autumn sky. Even Flavia was taken aback by it all, but felt no pleasure in the fact that she would now be paid slightly more for doing nothing than she had been for working flat out for years. What she had had to do to reach this state weighed on her, and the fact that nothing whatsoever could have been done to change the situation made it no better.

She packed up her office, and then she and Argyll packed up their apartment after a short search to find a quiet house about thirty kilometers outside Florence, a little way out of a lovely village that still had some Italians living in it. There, as the months passed, and she waddled more and her feet swelled up, the contentment returned, little by little. She painted her new kitchen. Chose curtains. Cooked and canned and froze. Sat quietly and dozed in the shade for longer and longer.

Argyll did his own form of nesting. He irritated Flavia mightily by fussing over her quite unnecessarily, giving her long scolding looks if she walked more than a hundred meters without taking a rest. He took to studying passing infants in strollers to see what they were like, receiving little in return except screams from the infants and suspicious looks from their mothers. He resigned from his job just in time to avoid having to give his fatuous paper on collecting, and, finally, waved good-bye to his pictures on the truck taking them to London. Then he followed them so that he could attend the sale. In between he revisited Bottando's picture, and sweet-talked Flavia's friend Aldo into letting him into the secret collection of the Vatican. When he saw it, he almost laughed, until he realized how all these pictures must have got there. Perfectly obvious, it was, when they were seen together. Add that to the drawing in the Uffizi, and he didn't even need Bulovius's notes.

The sale was a splendid success. Thanks to Mary Verney bidding frequently through several intermediaries and paying cash afterward, the four separate auctions in which Argyll's pictures came up established a minor legend in the art trade. At the same time, Argyll's stock soared as a man evidently cleverer than he seemed. Each picture shot through the estimate and climbed to dizzying heights. A pencil sketch by Rossini: estimate £200, sold for £3,500. A small oil on panel, *Descent from the Cross,* by Cantarini: estimate £1,500, sold for £14,500.

On it went. Seventy-three lots, and by the time the last was sold, an acceptable portion of the ransom money had been washed, cleaned, and ironed through the auction houses' financial departments, and transferred into Argyll's bank account. Mary Verney was substantially poorer and in possession of several dozen minor pictures for which she had no room whatsoever.

And while he was in London for an exhibition opening party at Edward Byrnes's gallery, Argyll mentioned that he and Flavia, with Bottando as well, maybe, were thinking of setting up in business for themselves, looking for missing pictures in a discreet fashion for those nervous about calling in the police.

"Really?" said one old man, a collector of prints who lived in the far north of Italy, near the Austrian Alps. Argyll had known him vaguely for years and had long liked him. "In that case, perhaps I might consult you over a delicate matter that has been bothering me for some time . . ."

Argyll hesitated, then smiled. "Well, " he said. "We'll have to see. I'll let you know. First of all I have some business with the Vatican."

"Really?" the old man said again.

"Yes. A little matter of a triptych. Quite an important one."

"Really? Who by?"

Argyll smiled, considered, then whispered in his ear. The old man looked shocked, and recoiled.

"Good Lord," he said. "Really?"